The Mouse Oracle

The Mouse Oracle

Nikki Elst

VANTAGE PRESS
New York

FIRST EDITION

Published by Vantage Press, Inc.
419 Park Ave. South, New York, NY 10016

Manufactured in the United States of America
ISBN: 0-533-15079-5

Library of Congress Catalog Card No.: 2004098075

0 9 8 7 6 5 4 3 2 1

To my family and friends
in heaven and here on Earth.

Thanks for sharing the wonderful journey with me. What
a gratifying experience!

The Mouse Oracle

1

You are only what you are when no one is looking.
—Abraham Lincoln

...Voices, echoing sounds...heavy footfalls...clicking rifles...fertig...ziehlen...schiessen...jawohl Herr Kommandant...tot...tot...maddening noises swirling in my head. I hear everything, everything. The German soldiers' goose-steps...the guns loading, the kommandant's command to fire. Everything...even the moon sighing in the sky.

A pitch black night with a crescent moon over San Francisco was the mise-en-scène for the nightmare that caught me bathed in cold sweat, writhing in agony and gasping for air. A terrible rage welled up inside me as I saw myself before the German firing squad with guns drawn, certain I was to be shot. I cannot say exactly why I was sentenced to death. I cannot even remember where the place was. I watched and listened, hoping the soldiers would go away and the nightmare would end as mysteriously as it had begun. But the dream continued mockingly. In fact, it grew scarier and scarier, leaving my knees in painful knots and my feet sticking up at the end of the bed like two ice needles.

The following morning when I awoke the early sun had settled on the surrounding houses, turning their pinkish pantiles bright red. But as the morning progressed, I told myself I have to get up at once and look for happiness.

Despite the sun's enthusiasm and my sense of well-being, it felt as though there was no life in me. Because the nightmare—so strangely fresh in my memory—was quietly preying on my mind, dimming all hopes that something wonderful was bound to happen, maybe even today . . . my birthday.

Oh dear! Oh dear! I heard myself saying. *Can it be that a message was contained in the dream that I failed to understand? Is some unforeseen danger lying in wait? Am I going to be killed and thrown into some dreary chasm to be devoured into oblivion? Be honest, God, and tell me— do I deserve such a fate?*

Many dreams have played on the stage of my mind in nameless acts. Some were bewildering to the mind and the emotions, and others as dark and gloomy as a miserable abyss where each step takes you further and further into a bottomless pit untouched by man or demon. I can compare last night's nightmare to one's feeling in a hurricane when one expects the ship to go down at any moment—while you lie awake all wrung out, your stomach in knots, your heart in your throat and lungs panting.

Sometime in the morning of the same day, something on top of the pond, not quite covered by the water lilies, flashed in the rays of the sun. It caught my eye, for it was the reflection of the Will of God written on my forehead. That image inspired me into a novel kind of action. *Hey, you! Snap out of it*, I told myself and tried to laugh away my fears. Feeling rather happy I concluded that perhaps the nightmare was nothing more than the monumental mockery of some freakish god bent on scaring me. It was a good try in the golden glow of the morning, brushed with blue.

The mind behind the eye sees that no matter how confusing the dream was, it had the earmark to become a high dramatic point in the annals of my most hated nightmares. How I loathed those creepy dreams, for they overshadowed the memory of my magical childhood reveries, in which I saw Godlike creatures on handsome white stallions, characters typically found in Hans Christian Andersen tales. I am beholden to those divine beings who rode on moonbeams to come to my room, to take me away to some faraway place, as immeasurably distant as the sky, where every day was a holiday with lots of balloons and bird-of-paradise feathers.

In later years, I reflected on those happy dreams, saying it was the sort of fantasy that would enchant almost any child; imaginative enough to walk on clouds.

In the world of fantasy, I would have been immortal for having my very own Oz, a blissfully joyous place with an amazing cast of characters.

I am not someone who necessarily believes in fairies and fairyland—an enchanting place that is virtually terra incognito to most people. However, this imaginary Never-never-land is one of the places—if there were a fairyland—to which I would like to return.

While nostalgia is at its zenith, let me take you back to that wondrous day in early June 1924 if only for a brief period to pretend that we are at Clouds, our palatial home in San Francisco, California, to celebrate a rite of passage. In other words; my twenty-first birthday.

Because Clouds is where my story begins.

No record exists of the birthday party at Clouds. But there is an anonymous 1924 photograph showing guests descending on Clouds like locusts, on the afternoon of June 8. It is so entirely of its time, boasting a signpost etched in boldface—CLOUDS—a tribute to my granddad,

Charles Theodore Grant, who was an American grandee of the Gold Rush era.

I see it all again in a wordless reverie—like clouds meeting their own reflections in water: the magnificent carriages with sleek horses, the shiny black cars with uniformed chauffeurs, gorgeous ladies resplendent in flowing silk gowns—each one more beautiful than the other—some shockingly low-necked; exposing bosoms glowing with scented rose balm. Indeed, I shall long remember the elegant men in black, their hair smooth and shiny with a touch of Brilliantine, and jewels so brilliant that they sparkled even in the bright glow of the flaming sunset.

Among many beautiful objects, I see myself in a portrait as I appeared at twenty-one, dressed in an iridescent blue gown that Coco Chanel had designed for me. The portrait was more impressive than it should have been. But, you see, it was painted by James Wythe Walker, whose passion was to paint with bold strokes the reigning beauties of the day.

Let me begin by introducing the guest oracle, Mme. Nomina Kappa and her mice. An ethereal creature, who on that day wore a silk-mousseline dress, exploding with the entire spectrum of blue, her lustrous black hair cascading insouciantly onto her shoulders, her mammoth black eyes stalking the room, as if wanting to unlock each door and take you inside.

In my mind, Mme. Kappa was identifiable with witches, who were evil spirits capable of putting magic spells on anyone they wished. Hence, I'm not sure why she was at the party, but something told me Mother, who loved to dabble in the occult, like the rest of her soigné coterie, had something to do with it. Despite Mme. Kappa's popularity, her past was a well-guarded secret;

padlocked with an iron lock. None knew whether she came from the great plains, the dense forests, the swampy valleys, or the high mountain ranges of Africa. A few brave hearts had a suspicion that she was born in deep Mississippi to a very poor Negro family that stayed alive because she had a gift. She could tell fortunes better than anyone else in that neck of the woods. So, I wasn't too surprised when she uttered the following words that, in time, were to change the threads of my destiny:

"*Mes amis* . . . here is *le resultat. Vraiment je regrette* to disappoint you but, you see, the spirits, who spoke through the mice, chose only one of you," Mme. Kappa said, combining French and English and a sprinkling of Italian for good measure. Her somber eyes and her deep throaty voice were reasons enough for me to want to leap into the large painting of the California desert hanging on the wall, hitch myself to a sturdy horse and disappear deep into the past, to a time when caravans of camels carried goods overland in California's southwest desert.

"*Oui* . . . Summer . . . it is you, my *cherie* whom the spirits favored." Mme. Kappa continued, peering into a strange looking gizmo—an African Mouse Oracle; an urn guarded by a human figure and now lined with new patterns of sticks, to foretell my future. I can still feel the chill that urn sent through me. Because, growing up in San Francisco, I was never exposed to African art per se. I was strictly raised on eighteenth century European and Asian art and furniture that had once graced the salons of royalty.

I recall my struggle with apathy, for I had this strange feeling that some bad fortune was lying in wait and it would spring to its feet at any moment, demanding human sacrifices to turn the tide.

"*Ma cherie, je parle la vérité,*" Mme. Kappa said ever

5

so softly, petting her sleeping oracles. In short, mice. As always her mannerism was absolutely perfect, worthy to be admired and funny to boot.

"Summer... mignonne, my darling... your future in San Francisco is a catalog of misery," she continued without eye contact as if speaking to a faceless cipher. I sensed immediately that something was terribly wrong, but I didn't yet know what. Good grief! Now I had a bigger hole in my gut than the one I had started with. "And... *la misère* has a voracious appetite. *Mi spiace*," she added in her own inimitable African style.

Sticks and stones can break my bones but words can never hurt me, I thought quietly, waiting for the next wave to hit me. "In order to reverse your destiny, you must leave your beloved San Francisco. *Oui*, yes, this is terrible but, on the other hand, treat it as a new challenge begging to be conquered. That way you can nip misfortune in the bud," she said, her voice cutting through the air as if on knife-edge.

The piquancy of her words, spoken so nakedly, got my dander up. Believe me, this foretold future was a little more than I had bargained for, especially on this day when I was disencumbering myself from my youth and joining the ranks of adulthood. I tried to speak, but my voice could hardly struggle through my parched throat. In the space of a few minutes, I had stepped from the twentieth century back several centuries, to an era when people were obsessed by witchcraft, and believed that witches influenced every facet of life. Now, feeling like one who had just bitten into a sour lemon, I managed to manipulate my lips by bribing my tongue to utter a few words apropos to the on-going conversation.

"Fiddlesticks! No one knows me better than the me inside me. And for all the gold in the U.S. Treasury, I cannot be persuaded to leave San Francisco, merely because a mouse said so," I snapped, eying Mother, the breathlessly elegant Annabel Grant, now in a state of severe agitation, barely able to overcome the gravity pull of the moment.

"*Cherie*... please try to remain calm. You cannot run away from your destiny. It will follow you wherever you go. The spirits—whether you believe in them or not—are providing you an insight into what the rest of your life is all about. Who knows... maybe you could become a legend in your own lifetime," she returned prophetically.

To be honest, I was confused and angry. What I didn't understand was how a silly mouse that thinks it is an oracle can foretell the future. This was too wild, too on the edge for my liking. This ado about nothing was, in fact, an insult to my intellect and, probably most important of all, my values were quite different than those of a small beastie with a long tail and small ears.

But while I continued to think of the mouse as something silly, the party itself was magical. The champagne and the music never stopped. You see, back in the early twenties, people really did outdo themselves with parties. The elegant guests, who came expecting magic, dressed in glamorous gowns adorned with diamonds, sapphires, and rubies, had found everything that they had wished for. Hence they saw no reason to concern themselves with the mouse. Yet, a few of my friends looked uneasy in their gorgeous fineries—you could easily imagine being transported to the eighteenth century—when hundreds of lovely women in silk taffeta and dripping with precious jewels would have danced in ballrooms as magnificent as Clouds'. Despite my effort to bring the focus to the far side of the fence, there was no escaping Mme. Kappa's words, as if spoken by the Priestess of the Python in

Africa, where she exists in many forms. Mme. Kappa's words clung to me not only like hungry leeches, but also like a venomous snake ready to wrap its body around my neck.

Now possessed by dark phantoms, I approached Mme. Kappa. "Madame, with all due respect, I honestly don't believe in your mice's ability to foretell one's future with a handful of small twigs placed in an urn. That's totally absurd, if you ask me. This is like practicing medicine without a license. On the other hand, let's say for the sake of argument, if there were any bit of truth in what you just said, good heavens! I don't want to bite the hand that fed me," I said calmly, but the fire in my blue eyes probably betrayed my anger.

"My dear girl ... quite honestly there are but a few good oracles in existence that would tell otherwise. So ... weigh the pros and the cons ... and ask yourself whether the whole of your happiness rests on a lie or the truth. Wait a few days; let your heart be your guide. Regardless of what you decide, you must go along with your destiny," Mme. Kappa replied, her mouth twitching for no apparent reason. "Now probably this will make no sense to you, because destiny wants what it wants and when it wants it. It's as simple as ABC. You cannot erase God's handwriting on your forehead, there since conception," Mme. Kappa explained and pushed me further into the abyss. "You are a day older than yesterday, but also much wiser. Time now to set the stage for forthcoming events that involve not only you, but your entire life."

The ensuing days were filled with anxiety, soul searching and self-hate for having acquired such a miserable destiny, through no fault of mine. God! Oh, God, why couldn't I have been blessed with a comfortable future that included a house with a white picket fence, flowers in the garden, chickens in the coop, birds in the trees and horses in the barn? In addition, a loving husband, beautiful children and a dozen or so Jack Russels to love me. Yes, God, that would be a destiny worthy of me.

And then it happened. Though why it did I cannot tell, even to myself. For whatever reason, I received a letter postmarked Constantinople, Turkey. It was eloquently written by my Uncle Hugh, my father's strikingly handsome brother, whom I adored with every fiber of my being.

Way back in the dark ages—when I was a sapling with eyes bigger than my head—I used to wonder about a lot of things that I didn't understand. Occasionally answers trickled back in surprising ways, then the enchantment was enormous. All this curiosity was bound to lead to trouble. But that didn't stop me from wondering why I loved Uncle Hugh more than I thought was proper. Did I love him because I thought of him as a grand illusion, who was always in the pulse of whatever excitement was going on in San Francisco, let alone in the world? Or did I love him because I wanted to be one of the accepted members of the cult that surrounded him?

Uncle Hugh's legendary adventures: big game in Africa, birds in South America, mammals in the Galapagos Islands, and his numerous liaisons with some of the most beautiful women of that era were, without a doubt, the source of curiosity and the gossip of the male bastion, The Bohemian Club, when the elite members gathered for their annual hiatus. Obviously, a much idolized man, he was seen as a figure to be emulated—much as star athletes are today. Maybe I was too young to understand all this, but you have no idea what I did see, what I did hear, what I did take in . . . despite my age.

If I seem uninspired by Uncle Hugh's letter, it's

because the content was so unreal. Uncle Hugh, who often used his Lothario looks to get what he wanted, was now asking me, *moi*, the debutante of the year, with a hundred thousand dollars annually for spending money, to drop everything in San Francisco and join him in Constantinople. This was absurd. He had to be kidding, *nest-ce-pa*s?

According to Uncle Hugh, the American colony in exile needed volunteers to help them raise money for the Russian refugees of the Bolshevik Revolution: aristocrats, officers of the Chevalier Garde, of the Semeonovski and Preobrajenski Garde regiments, intelligentsia, soldiers, and simple peasants who were arriving at Constantinople in a steady stream, carrying with them only few belongings, but many memories of the Mother Russia they once knew.

After many years dreaming of dreams bigger than life itself, it was only proper that my mind should work rapidly to allow me a glimpse of myself on the arm of Uncle Hugh, making a big splash in the Ottoman City, wearing a gossamer silk dress with rhinestones and bugle beads cascading down the back, like water from a spigot.

That entire day, I fiddled with the letter, reading it over and over, pondering whether to go or not to go. I told myself—as if talking to a halfwit—one has to be an absolute ninny to pass up such a golden opportunity to visit the legendary Sultans' paradise. Yet, despite the Ottoman enticement, I hesitated. You, reader, must wonder why someone didn't check me immediately into a funny farm. This was a golden opportunity that I was throwing away. But, let me explain. Though I was only twenty-one, a big part of me was very old, because my family's deep roots traced back to George Washington and

Colonial times. That alone was a heavy responsibility by itself for any young person of a noble family.

And to be honest, I simply didn't want to leave Clouds. As far back as I can remember, an extraordinary bond existed between Clouds and me, which took on a special importance—partly because it teased the imagination, partly because it was the folly of my granddad, an icon of his era. Clouds was designed to resemble a French chateau with lobate windows and balconies at the three upper levels, intended to give the building the appearance of belonging more to Loire than San Francisco, a city by the Bay that boasted many grandiose houses, built in an era of ever-changing moods when architects, vying to outdo each other in size and in originality, created architectural follies with up-up-up magic for San Francisco's first families that applied a lot of gingerbread on their homes without inhibition.

Also, I knew next to nothing about quixotic pursuits. The repertoire of my achievements was somewhat limited and a complete list of those accomplishments would barely fill a paragraph, let alone a page. Much of my life in San Francisco consisted of supporting local cultural institutions and serving as a volunteer at the local chapter of the American Red Cross. Hardly wildly exciting stuff for a girl my age. But, you see, in earlier days, only a few young ladies of good family went to work after graduating from high school. And going to a university was almost unheard of; for most women marriage remained the parachute of choice.

During the following weeks, I lived with the constant echo of Mme. Kappa's now infamous words: "Your future in San Francisco is a catalog of misery." Despite the warning and the dread of catastrophic tomorrows, I couldn't picture myself in Turkey, a country where women constituted a lower order of being. I believe it was the Duke of Wellington who said, looking at his troops: "I don't know what effect these men will have on the enemy, but, my God, they terrify me." And, by God, the Ottoman Empire, perhaps the greatest empire in the world, filled me with terror. But let me leave the discussion of terror for a later chapter.

In my mind, Constantinople, one of the most beautiful cities in the world with its trinity of names: Byzantium, Constantinople, Ottoman City; its Golden Horn, Bosphorus, Marmara Sea, the Grand Seraglio, and its cast of characters from the Arabian Nights held no interest for me whatsoever, and was never a top priority destination on my list of cities that I wanted to see. London, Paris, Rome, Brussels and Madrid were places for big-time stuff. And the ultimate truth was, I didn't want to roam so far from my ancestral home.

For me, my ancestral home, Clouds, was the first enchanted place of my life—endlessly dear and lost forevermore—where I spent some of the happiest times of my childhood. Situated on a high rise atop Nob Hill, Clouds commanded a wide vista on all sides, yet allowed the other houses, equally unique, to shine all on their own, on this ideal site that provided the setting for so many magnificent parties.

If a common denominator united all those San Franciscan follies, it was their lavish households with English butlers, Chinese cooks, and a variety of servants from housemaids to laundry maids. In addition, these establishments had English and German governesses and nurses—not to mention the chauffeurs, the gardeners and other outdoor staff whose task was to create a country atmosphere in the heart of a city that never slept.

However, somehow or other, Mme. Kappa's seeds of fear had rooted themselves in my brain and were acting like hungry leeches snuffing out all sensation from the rest of my body. Thus, after considering such options as joining the Bohemians in Paris, slumming in Montmartre, living among the giant gorillas in Africa, teaching at a remote school somewhere in Asia, or working at the Belgian Consulate in Zanzibar, I jumped assuredly on my own bandwagon and opted for Constantinople and the humanitarian mission, hoping to have fun in the process.

If I recall correctly, it was at that time that my decision to leave San Francisco and my beloved Clouds became the hottest topic making the rounds of the city's electric chi-chi salons. Keep in mind that in the early twenties, most spinsters lived almost always at the parental home with its own absorbing inner life: surrounded by lush gardens with hundreds of urns filled with cascading bright petunias and white geraniums and where tea, freshly churned ice cream and a medley of delicate cookies were served on Tiffany china, under scented pavilions, smothered in alabaster-colored roses. Hence no one, in her right mind, was too anxious to give up a tenure in paradise for the discomfort of the small bachelor girl's apartment.

An old journal tells me that on the evening of March 6, 1923, Uncle Hugh dropped one of the biggest bombshells on the Grant family. (Trust me on this.) It was a bombshell powerful enough to create a jolt as mighty as a deadly earthquake reading 8.9 on the Richter scale. Were we stunned? You bet we were, but not surprised. Because so often, Uncle Hugh took us on paths that we never intended to travel, yet we always ended up enjoying the ride.

I can only suppose that Uncle Hugh had the following speech in his mind for a long time. I doubt that such a speech could have been delivered on the spur of the moment.

"I've been lucky to have wealth and the success that I had," Uncle Hugh said in a strong voice echoing with self-confidence. It was the same type of confidence that he shared with his Colt pistol, always within reach.

"Yes, family, you are about all the things that I love. That's what's most important to me. However, *noblesse oblige*. Hence, I've decided, after a long debate with my conscience, to go to Constantinople to spearhead a private non-profit American organization with a well-organized staff that knows Constantinople from one end to the other. The organization's sole goal will be to help the White Army under my friend General Wrangel. During this time of chaos and famine, and soldiers in rags, he needs me. I just can't ignore his pleas for help any longer. I have to fish, or cut bait, as they say. It is not a question of guilt so much as one of common decency. Perhaps, this is just a quixotic gallantry to protect them from being massacred by the Bolsheviks who, presently, are ten times stronger than the Whites.

"However, after all is said and done, I believe it's my passion for danger that slingshots me to the upper spectrum of courage." That said, Uncle Hugh flashed one of his killer smiles, which made my heart skip a beat or two, and left the room, humming one of John Phillip Sousa's marches.

That dramatic backdrop framed the tragedy of errors that followed.

2

It seemed to me that while other cities are mortal
Constantinople will endure as long as there are
men on earth.
　　　—Petrus Gyllius, in the 16th century

It may seem strange, but fifty years ago almost to the day,
I left San Francisco to embark on a kind of life about
which I knew nothing. The whole of that day—July 2,
1925—is like a jigsaw puzzle with pieces missing. However, I have a vague memory of myself sitting in a car,
close by my dad, his face masked with a veil of sadness,
who was chauffeuring me to the station on that summery
day in San Francisco with the fog slithering into the Bay,
and the cable cars rattling and creaking up Nob Hill,
their bells almost echoing my mother's parting words.
"Please don't leave. You haven't got what it takes to go on
your own. You'll fall flat on your face."

I smile as I recall the way Daddy struggled with my
various Louis Vuitton portmanteau trunks—massive
brown cubes with brass mountings, train cases and hat-
boxes in Epi leather with my own initials, because during
the golden age of travel, the fashionable gentility didn't
take two tiny carryalls like today on a plane.

The agony of having to say good-bye is an emotion I
always find hard to deal with. But now with those beck-
oning voices of Turkey resonating before me the agony of
parting was slowly diminishing to the point of non-exis-

tence. It was all quite unusual. Not only was I going to a place I had never been before; I was also traveling solo in the company of people as mysterious as the beings on Mars.

This was the ultimate freedom . . . This was like leaping a horse over a wall with the wind behind.

Once on the train, despite my sense of loneliness, I experienced a feeling of great joy. I'd been dreaming of this day and now felt as if someone had flung open a door allowing me to embark on a new life with my newly sprouted wings. This was something miraculous, something beyond magic. Yet, as I stood at the window, my face close to the pane, looking back toward the beloved city I had just left, to the glitzy world of *haut monde* that once was mine, my chest heaved with emotion—like an animal being taken to the slaughterhouse. What I felt was similar to the feeling I'd had, as a child, on the first day of kindergarten.

It so happened that I loved trains. Many wonderful tales and songs have been written and sung about all sorts of trains. Romantic . . . well . . . maybe. But keep in mind, despite the train's mystique, it took one so long to get anywhere. The steady rhythms of the wheels, fast and changing scenes, and nights that grew longer were constant reminders that in front of me lay a journey of four days on the Overland Limited to Chicago, plus a day on the Twentieth Century Limited to New York. It took seven days on the Cunard to reach France. Then an additional eighty-four hours aboard the Simplon-Orient Express to reach Constantinople from Paris. It all seemed endlessly long. How awful is the slow passing of time when one is twenty-two and impatient.

However, before I reach my destination, let me tell you how all this came about. I believe, sometime before I was born, I must have suggested to myself that after my presentation at Clouds (the San Francisco Cotillion was founded after the Depression) while other debutantes hoped to be asked to join the Junior League, or take their summers in Biarritz, Cannes, Maine or Sorrento on the Bay of Naples with their families, I would be among the fortunate few who would be dreaming about adventure. Now, at long last, I was fulfilling one of my life's goals. Like Mata Hari, the notorious Dutch Indonesian dancer and German spy, who often rode the Orient Express when on a spying mission, I too was riding the fabled train, rubbing elbows with fictional heroes: Sherlock Holmes and Hercule Poirot, as well as real-life royalty: Edward VIII of England and Prince Youssoupov of Russia, and famous authors: Edith Wharton, F. Scott Fitzgerald and Sergey Yesenin, the Russian poet and husband of Isadora Duncan—dining on ebony inlaid tables, off Mansard plates and drinking wine from monogrammed crystal goblets. Never have I experienced a more thoroughly enjoyable train ride.

It was mid-morning when the Orient Express pulled elegantly into the Sirkeci Station, a pseudo-Moorish building and the terminus of the fabulous train. I put down my flute of champagne and said good-bye to my fellow travelers, paying silent homage to all those adventurers that had come before and who, like us, rode the train across six frontiers to reach Constantinople.

How exotic appeared Constantinople! How extraordinary the skyline, how pervasive the spirit of Islam on that day in July 1925. However, what really awed my young eyes was the way a chain of gauzy clouds were veiling the golden domes and the tall minarets of giant sun-blanched mosques as if to protect them from the corroding tooth of time.

17

As I write these personal observations—yanked from my memory bank so carefully stored all these years—I try to imagine them in their vibrancy, and remember how easily my senses were whisked away into a state of instant Ottoman euphoria, and how little was required to visualize Sultans in ermine-trimmed robes, on their heads turbans with aigrettes of peacock feathers, riding handsome stallions, their saddles studded with precious gems. I chuckle, remembering my own three feathers on my head when I was presented to the society during the Gilded Age.

I was the first passenger out of the train—a stranger in the midst of strange people, speaking a mélange of accents and languages I could neither understand nor guess. I saw exotic men wearing red fezzes with long tassels. Women in billowy black dresses, their faces covered with veils—exposing only kohl-lined dark eyes. Young uniformed governesses herding their charges dressed in white dresses with bright sashes and flower-trimmed hats. White-gloved porters carrying the fine leather valises of the stylish voyagers—the exquisite cut of their clothes that would have done credit to the couture houses in Paris—if they had not in fact originated there in the first place. Old beggars in threadbare pants and shirts, looking for a few coins. These are just a few of the souvenirs of my arrival in Constantinople.

Meanwhile, I had to say good-bye to the Orient Express and transfer to a line that went due south. With a porter in tow pushing a cart heaped with my luggage, I moved to the next platform filled with various kiosks purveying newspapers, magazines, candies and nuts, all trying to snare weary passengers heading home in the evening.

I took a window seat in the first-class compartment

of a steam train that operated between Sirkeci Station and San Stefano—my final destination—and all the way to Kucuk Cekmece. I sank my body into a large brown leather seat (obviously meant for a giant with long legs) to let my pirouetting mind return to reality. Because arriving in the East from the West can, sometimes, be a mind-boggling experience not suitable for weak-kneed characters. By mere chance, an Italian woman of a certain age, her lovely face etched with lines from countless hours under the Mediterranean sun, sat on the seat across from mine. She was busy pouring out her heart to a man with an enviable bone structure resembling Rudolph Valentino, the greatest male heartthrob of the twentieth century. He seemed to have been a part of the lady's past, before life bore down on her. I tried to pierce the mystery of their conversation, but I didn't have a particularly good handle on the Italian language. Although I knew a few simple words, these weren't enough to understand the libretto of the unfolding Italian opera.

At times when the conversation approached a crescendo, I lent my ears to two elderly ladies who were busy discussing the price of rose-petal and green-fig jam, and didn't seem to care about the ongoing Italian drama. Next to them a young couple sat holding hands timidly, their eyes heavy with sleep.

As for me, well... I was another pair of gloves. I had nothing better to do but cast furtive glances at the resplendent landscape of rolling hills with seaside villages—some as old as time itself, some ablaze with blood-red showy geraniums, some buried under yellow honeysuckle, and others lined with row after row of drying silvery mackerel—all releasing their own brand of rich scents, not something that is necessarily appreciated by Westerners.

Gradually, the steady, hypnotic *clickety-clack* of the wheels changed to an almost lulling sound. All around me passengers, as varied as their tongues, were gathering their belongings and preparing themselves to leave the train at the next stop; which would be San Stefano, Uncle Hugh's idyll by the Marmara Sea. As I began to put my baggage in order, the train shook suddenly and came to a screechy halt, scattering boxes, newspapers and children from one end of the compartment to the other.

From the sound of anxious voices, it was quite apparent the locomotive had hit something—or *someone.* I opened the capacious window and stuck my head out to see what was going on. I heard the trees soughing in the wind and I saw the afternoon sun resting on the flowers that could not have been more ethereal. Yet, I sensed a flow in what I saw. Fearing a terrible mishap, I threaded myself between the passengers and stepped outside.

No one was there to greet me. I saw only the scarlet heads of the poppies.

The sound of crushed gravel, the *churr* of the insects in the tall weeds, the cry of a lone crow and the scent of the acacia trees floating in the air were the sounds and the smell that welcomed me to San Stefano on that exceptionally beautiful day; all contributing to imprint my memory.

Anxious with fear (an emotion we share with animals when they smell danger somewhere) I ran toward the locomotive which was still hissing on the tracks. On the heavy gravel strewn between the tracks lay a shapeless black bundle. Closer examination revealed the body of a woman in a black moiré chemise and salvar (bouffant pantaloons) to match. Her childlike face was wound tightly with a veil, exposing only the brow and the eyes. A few young porters were eyeing her motionless body like vultures gathering to feast on the rotting flesh from another animal's kill. People young and old were moving in and out of the train cars wondering what to do. A few passengers hurried along, bound on some mission, oblivious to the body shimmering in the sun like a sea serpent with shiny scales. Everything else continued as it always had.

I can honestly say I had never beheld a sight more disturbing, one which made my blood freeze. Some people are repelled by the thought of death. I am one of them. Yet, as I walked toward the prone woman now in the throes of death, I felt relatively calm. I bent over the body and held my breath, to ascertain whether she was breathing or not. She was barely alive. I cradled her torso in my arms and rocked it gently, hearing the grating sound of broken bones. Just for an instant her lips moved faintly as if wanting to say something. Then I heard the death rattle in her throat. I prayed that God would get on with it and take her soul into His Kingdom. Then she was gone, leaving behind her flesh, impregnated with amber perfumes. Her once beautiful dark eyes were now opaque, staring at the sky like colorless flames. I closed her eyelids, pressed a coin into her palm, for the journey ahead, and dried my tears. Suddenly, a bird, perhaps, and Bulbul (nightingale) appeared from nowhere and vanished into the trees beyond. Another soul had begun its long journey.

"*Oldu, oldu, kiz oldu. Gidin, Gidin*" (Dead, dead, the girl is dead. Go away, go away), repeated a stocky man wearing what appeared to be the uniform of a station master. He was trying to disperse the group of curious hangers-on, who seemed to be totally blasé about this assumed suicide, which, I later learned, was a common occurrence in this part of the world.

Little by little the people left, shaking their heads in wonder. I don't remember how long I stood there, impatiently pacing and yawning while waiting for a summoned ambulance that never came. Nor did the police arrive to take a report from the locomotive engineer. Endless discussions punctuated with smoking cigarettes took place but no one was deemed responsible for the woman's death or provided her body with medical attention. Her death was merely death; nothing more, nothing less. The only thing that everyone agreed was that her death was a tragedy, like the women of dramatic literature before her, perhaps influenced by Tolstoy's *Anna Karenina*. Who can ever forget that fictional character's desperate final act when she throws herself in front of the train? This young woman too threw herself in front of the locomotive, evidently believing that death is better than the continuance of intolerable suffering.

As I made my way back to the train car to fetch my luggage, I was overcome with the strange sensation that I had grown older during the span of an hour. I ran my hand over my face to feel if I had developed a wrinkle or two that weren't there before. Suddenly, I heard heavy footfalls ensuing, almost quivering the ground before me. Then I heard a man's voice.

"Miss, please wait," he pleaded. "Don't be frightened. I just want to talk to you. I have something here that I believe belongs to you." I turned around to see who was speaking. It was the station master holding a small something in his hand.

"Well... what is it? I don't remember losing anything," I said.

"I'm not sure whether this belongs to you, but look at it anyway," the station master persisted, puffing on a foul-smelling cigarette.

"Well, all right. Let me see it. Whatever this is, I assure you it's not mine. In fact, I've never seen anything like it. Good-bye," I grunted. By then I was tired and had endured more than a bellyful of the harsh realities of life in Turkey. From the looks of things, it seemed as if the catalog of misery had already found its way to Constantinople.

"Tell me, please . . . if this amulet belongs to you?" the station master asked again, but this time more demandingly. Then he handed me the round, blue glass eye. I honestly didn't know what to make of it.

"I've already told you, this doesn't belong to me. Perhaps it belonged to the deceased girl," I said, examining the eye carefully.

"I found it at the very spot where you were standing. So I assumed the eye was yours."

"It's a lovely charm, to say the least, but it's not mine. Really. What do you suppose it is?" I asked now that my curiosity was circling over the glass eye like a homeless bee.

"Here in Turkey—in fact in most Muslim countries— superstitious people swear that the blue eye possesses magical power to ward off evil spirits. Go ahead and keep it. Consider it a gift from a good fairy. Better yet, think of it as a talisman to keep away evil."

"Well, okay. Who knows, maybe someday I will look upon this as a good omen," I said and popped the eye into my pocket. I felt silly and thought, *Why, that's the silliest thing I've ever done.* But, on the other hand, it was amusing that now I owned a good luck charm without the benefit of a good fairy, but only because of the death of a total stranger, who died in my arms. Was this blue eye her last act of kindness? If I knew, maybe we all might stop wondering and adjust ourselves to the ways of the East.

Though lifeless, the glass eye seemed to have an energy all of its own. I could almost feel it pulsating against my skin. Consumed with a double dose of curiosity, I tried to recreate and play back in slow motion the tragic scenario that I had just witnessed, hoping to capture a small detail that I could have overlooked. Just the sheer thought of it brought on a bad case of goose-bumps. In spite of the unfortunate incident, I knew I would be okay and the sun would rise again in its majesty. Because death with all its dark labyrinths hadn't ruined anything for me. I was still breathing, my skin felt warm, and I was in San Stefano.

I'm rarely at a loss for words. But it happened to me on that day in San Stefano when I found myself totally defenseless at the sight of shafts of sunlight slanting down from blooming Judas trees creating a kaleidoscope of colorful patterns on the pavement. It was so simple, yet so magnificent. That afternoon God had outdone Himself in a big way.

Before I could give the coachman the address, he drove off with a nonchalant twirl of his whip, as if he had read my mind. The black phaeton, drawn by a young gelding, made a graceful mid-street turn and followed a paved road covered with dusty potholes from countless years of neglect. The coachman, a chain-smoker, lazily flicked the reins, enveloped in a cloud of smoke. At one point, he came to life as he coaxed the horse to climb a steep hill. The animal hesitated for a few minutes but it continued, despite a grade that was clearly too steep for its liking.

Well ... hello, San Stefano!

It was a lovely afternoon with red poppies, blue lupines, yellow buttercups and other wild flowers carpeting San Stefano's roadsides. I relaxed against the leather back seat and took a deep breath to inhale the surrounding scent, which turned out to be the perfume of the Yonder bush. My Lord! How menacingly beautiful they were. It was hard to imagine that these bushes bearing such lovely flowers were the very same branches used for the crown of thorns worn by Christ on the day of his crucifixion. Isn't it ironic that the same God who made the lovely flowers had also made the sharp thorns?

To this day the reality of His creation remains puzzle enough.

After several miles of breathless scenery, the air heavy with the scent of ripe figs and blooming acacias, the horse trotted through a large iron gate, embellished with sea-horse handles. I was instantly mesmerized by their beauty. The horse continued over a bright carpet of wildflowers muffling its hoof beats. Ahead of us and beyond an assemblage of umbrella pines, an illusion of a house glistened in the sun's rosy afterglow, its walls splashed with a rainbow of color, like a child's conception of a castle in a fairy tale. I oohed and aahed about the scenery.

When the driver heard my exuberant joy, he shrugged his shoulders nonchalantly and said, "Oh, that's the Italian House. It's haunted by the ghost of Amelia Chioggia. Luckily for the villagers, all her life Amelia had also loved to gossip. So San Stefano's coffers are full of her stories. Now . . . she is a friendly ghost, who still thinks the house belongs to her." I smiled at the driver and he smiled back shaking his head and mumbling to himself.

Against all odds, I shouldn't be here! Yet here I was, in the middle of nowhere, going to a haunted house. Then it dawned on me. This house flaunting itself with such abandon could be none other than "Mon Plaisir," Uncle Hugh's enchanting hideaway in equally enchanting San Stefano.

Even more interesting to me was the fact that Mon Plaisir was the fancy (or maybe the folly?) of a woman named Amelia Chioggia, an admitted Francophile Italian, who was a friend of Armand Henri Favre, the French painter known for his still-life oils and collages. Her dream was to live on this tongue of land, surrounded with water and roses that were in vogue in the early 1900s. I loved roses too. Amelia's ghost might be a kindred spirit, after all.

Houses like Mon Plaisir warrant ghost stories. Mon Plaisir has that and some more. The locals love to regale the curious visitors and the aficionados of the paranormal with their own version of the story, which isn't too far off from the truth. But . . . what is the truth? A storm? A wind? The sea? Or was it destiny? No way to be sure. Who cares, really?

Locally the tragic tale is told with a certain irony: "During a storm when the wind howled like a demented soul and giant waves crashed with a thunderous roar, a sudden gust of wind blew Amelia into the sea and the sea swallowed her without leaving a trace. Now, on balmy nights when the fireflies dance in the bushes, if one listens good and hard, one can almost hear a whistle—like a birdcall—wafting from the sea. We call this lovely phenomenon 'Amelia's Cry.'"

Finally, Amelia's heirs in Italy sold the property to Uncle Hugh, who himself was a romantic at its most recherché. It was a love match right from the start. And Mon Plaisir became a folly for a second time. Lovely Amelia had found her match in Uncle Hugh.

For many this story is simply another fiber in the colorful tapestry of San Stefano—once the idyll of Constantine—the Byzantine Emperor, son of Constantius I and St. Helena. Despite his mother's devotion to God, he himself was baptized only on his deathbed.

But for me the legend of Mon Plaisir is all too real . . . because I experienced Mon Plaisir.

3

I have seen the ruins of Athens, of Ephesus, and of
Delphi. But I never beheld a work of nature which
yielded an impression like the prospect on each
side, from the Seven Towers to the end of the
Golden Horn.
—Lord Byron, 1810

Happily for me, the trip so far had been pleasant with
exceedingly pretty scenery. Suddenly pretty became magical when, for the first time, I saw Mon Plaisir up close.
She was a beautiful enchantress that cast a spell over me,
immediately. She bathed me in acacia perfume and
strewed blossoms, in every stage of growth, along my
path. This was puzzling, even to me.

Also, even more important, was a man called Monsieur Boris, Uncle Hugh's amiable butler, who considered
it a privilege to serve me. Once a Grand Duke, who ate
out of Fabergé bowls, now he was content to wear a peas-
ant's cotton shirt embroidered with blue cornflowers, a
thick back cord at the waist and trousers stuffed into
black boots.

In fairy tales, princesses live in castles surrounded
by winding lanes leading nowhere. In real life, I was
given the "Swallow's Nest," a two-room suite amid
shapely pines and draped in pink jasmine. It resembled
the original Swallow's Nest in Yalta, now crumbling on
its perch. Whatever its provenance, this was my castle

for a new set of dreams.

The interior of the Swallow's Nest fully lived up to its spectacular exterior. Overwhelmed with emotion, the eyes blink, the eyelashes flutter and the vocal chords twitch, as the senses acquaint themselves with Swallow's Nest's surrealistic interior's interpretation of the exotic spirit of an Oriental potentate. It was the first time ever that a house had spoken to me with such an Eastern voice: doors gleaming with layers of black lacquer, walls adorned with ancient tapestries. Chairs upholstered in pretty salmon-colored silk twill. Thick rugs right off the backs of Kashmir sheep. Hand-painted wallpaper in floral Chinoiserie design.

The main color of the rooms was a muted green, a fitting background to the mother-of-pearl inlaid bibliothèque crammed with ornate miniatures, and a collection of enameled boxes by Maria Samanova and Fabergé. In addition, it contained complete sets of the Russian masters: Chekhov, Dostoevsky, Pushkin, Turgenev and Leo Tolstoy. All this layering of colors, textiles, books and paintings had the earmark of a man who wanted the rooms to reflect his own passion. Boris had made Swallow's Nest itself a passion.

After a crash course in how to navigate in a labyrinthine city like Constantinople with streets barely wide enough for pedestrians, let alone pushcarts laden with everything under the sun—ranging from baked goods to old rugs, and well-to-do turbaned old men selling gold and silver plates, jeweled swords and daggers, embroidered capes and caps for young boys who must undergo circumcision at the age of ten. I was ready to take on Constantinople, et al. Fortunately for the gypsy street entertainers, I was not going near them. They were a free-born breed; no man could tell them how to lead their lives.

Now free of all confinements, and no longer restricted to one village, or city, I was assigned to manage Le Magasin Pomme d'Or, the American organization's gift shop in the heart of Pera, the chi-chi district of Constantinople. The Pomme d'Or's sole purpose was to help the White Russians, fleeing from the Bolsheviks. The shop was unique in so many ways. One beautiful art flowed into another—like the ceiling tiles dating from the seventeenth century, and the bronze tulip tree fountain, copied from one in the gardens of Peterhof Palace in St. Petersburg, beautiful touches that attracted hordes of people, out to feed their curiosity. And the fact that it was adjacent to The Japon Bazar, the most famous toy store in Constantinople, made the entire area a must-see address for children and for adults going on ten.

In my time, Pera was a postcard-perfect neighborhood, ablaze with glitterati and haunted by Ottoman ghosts. Nor was it surprising that it had the power to capture the imagination. In fact, many romances continued in and out of Pera, and it was there that the beautiful Flora Cordier, a Belgian modiste, had kept a shop that was frequented by Sultan Hamid himself, who often came to buy gloves and scarves, and to feast on the gossip fermenting under the pavement. Then, one day, Flora, captured by her own imagination, said, *"Pourquoi non,"* when Sultan Hamid asked if she would marry him. This is a realized fantasy, but the Sultan's Yildiz Palace was not in her future. Poor Flora was carted off to an obscure small house near the Byzantine land walls, where she waited in utter loneliness for an occasional order from her husband to visit him in his chamber at Yildiz, Abdul Hamid's sumptuous palace on the northern side of the Golden Gate.

Meanwhile, back in the United States, Americans

were enjoying the highest standard of living in the country's history. And in Germany, after the publication of Hitler's *Mein Kampf*, Hitler was calling for a national revival and war against Communism and Jews. This was the beginning of a massive witch-hunt for a man bent on controlling not only Germany, but the entire world.

In 1926, I reinvented myself. I enrolled in a program for secret agents at the British Embassy in Pera. It was a hush-hush operation conducted by the British Secret Service. Right from the start complete dedication and absolute silence was demanded. If captured you were countryless. Your fate: death.

As for me, the uncluttered simplicity of the program and the spirit of the unity were radical departures from the way I was brought up. I cannot say that I was intimidated by death. Because, as far as I can remember, the nightmares of the early years were almost always riddled with shootings, hangings, strangulations, and slashings.

During those years of political unrest in the world, people did their utmost to put their best faces forward: women rushed out to buy the popular flapper dresses with dropped waistlines, and Maurice Marinet's celebrated glass objects—all this while German soldiers were being trained in the USSR. The cinema, the theatre, and the circus were accepted antidotes to the time's plethora of rebarbative news, promoting fantasy in competition with other harsher realities.

On one perfect day in mid-August—when you could hear the ooze of the syrup escaping from the figs and the burst of the giant white mulberries—I oiled my body and stretched under the sun to make it more bronze. As I was searching for a scarf to cover my head, the phone rang. The casual observer might presume I was having a lovely conversation, but this was altogether different. Mr.

Phillip Page from the Secret Service was on the line to inform me that I had been chosen by the Agency to carry out an important task. This was a great honor, not so much because of the importance as because I, a peach plucked before her time, was to collaborate with the handsome and notorious German spy (code name Zulu) who intimidated almost everyone with his nose-bone. The sheer thought of meeting him petrified me. Yet I felt elevated, for I was no longer a member outside looking in. I had arrived! Despite my momentary high, I asked myself if my guts were tough enough to bring down a man at a close range? My answer surprised me.

Violent scenarios, so gruesome in my nightmares, came back to haunt me. I felt my blood escaping from my pores drop by drop. Just thinking about those dreams made me lose all confidence in myself. Back in my room, I sprinkled potassium cyanide crystals on a piece of candy, enough to kill myself, if captured.

Despite my trepidation, rubbery legs and the duels in my stomach, I psyched myself into believing that I wasn't in a death spiral. This was just a job that had to be done. Dressed in full glamour regalia, I mingled with all sorts of people out for a good time. With my wide-brimmed hat that hid half of my face, I resembled one of those incognitas of the night, who haunt the streets of Istanbul. It was hard to tell whether I was an ordinary woman with eccentric tendencies, or a prostitute in a cotton dress with a corset worn outside.

As I walked through the doors of the Pera Palace Hotel, I felt as if I were in a colony of elegant flies, the sound of their buzz magnified by their ability to work together in confined quarters. The uniformed doorman directed me to a blue room that was illuminated by a nineteenth-century crystal chandelier festooned with small roses. Once I settled myself in a big chair, I realized my imagination had caught fire. I was sure I was being watched by hundreds of eyes—slanted, round, small, big, green, blue and black—all staring at me through tiny holes in the woodwork. In reality, the room was empty except for me and two fat Angora cats sleeping on a silk sofa.

Soon I was caught up in the excitement of the mission; I heard male voices in the lobby. Bending down to admire a large crystal horse head, I was fascinated and terrified at the same time to see a face in the clear crystal. Moments later, the reflection disappeared. As I raised my head, I saw a man stubbing out a half-smoked cigarette with his thumb and simultaneously lighting a new one. Then I saw the nose-bone. Terror pursued terror. Zulu made a picturesque figure in a light gray suit, a small yellow rose in the boutonniere. He was tall with an erect carriage and an intellectual forehead strewn with freckles. He looked very smart. Obviously, he had dressed fashionably for the prospect of meeting a woman of fashion. Zulu was everything that I had imagined him to be; a man with all the grace of a panther.

You see, reader, Zulu wasn't your average spy, or for that matter, your average man. By chance, if you had found yourself in a museum, you would have seen a similar handsome face in one of John Singer Sargent's paintings.

"Wonderful . . . wonderful . . . you do have style, just as I thought. I love a spy of fashion," Zulu uttered in a throaty voice. He clutched my hand shyly. His grip was strong, yet soft. He took a chair close to mine and ordered two peach brandies over champagne. The whole scene was carefully orchestrated to give the prying eyes the impression that this was a friendly tête-à-tête.

"As you know, spies, like us, live by the code, which translates to: no friends, no emotions, no IDS, total isolation. We are programmable living robots. There are no heroes among spies! We do what we are told and ask no questions. It's not a favorable climate for friendships, it's a cloak-and-dagger existence. Still . . . if you are my enemy, I want to know it."

"I didn't come here as a foe. In fact, I like you, despite your reputation for hating women. I don't know what this is all about. I fully understand the dangers of coming here. But . . . it's a job that I must do," I said, firing my words with the accuracy of a pistol.

Zulu stared into the air and said nothing. He seemed unaware of what I had just said. In a sudden friendlier mood, after the traditional pleasantries had been exchanged, he offered me a cigarette from a silver case. However, prior to coming here, I was instructed to take two cigarettes simultaneously. Light one and drop the other one nonchalantly into my bag. That innocent cigarette, however, contained a secret message, written in invisible ink. At that point Zulu sent two long puffs of smoke into the air. In turn, I took several deep puffs of my cigarette, curling the smoke toward Zulu. These friendly exchanges of smoke puffs were to signal each other that the hunt was over and now we could clean our rifles.

"Agent, let me remind you . . . when I leave this room, I can no longer be of service. You don't know me. In fact, we never met. I'm a person who doesn't exist," Zulu said coldly. Then he was gone, in a silence as detached as his arrival.

The next morning the whole face of the sky was honeycombed with small clouds. The air was full of scents wafting from the garden. I felt as happy as an undug clam left in the shallows of the sea. I put away my gun and sank to my knees to thank the invisible God for sparing me from killing a man.

Later I was back at Pomme d'Or watching people who were busy watching each other—like hunting hawks. I felt a great sense of pride as they craned their necks to admire the miniatures painted by Captain Sergei Afonivich, a former officer of the Russian Imperial Guard, whose brothers Andre, Dimitri and Boris, all students at the Alexander Lyceum, were murdered. The beauty of the miniatures made the room's soft lights seem like a superfluous addition to an already good thing. Besides being a talented painter, Captain Afonivich also was a master sculptor, who created marvelous tiny chairs, tables, bureaus and armoires, all built to perfect scale. However, the star of his vast repertoire was "The Piano," a realistic small instrument, painted black with gleaming ivory keys, that left the most sophisticated, even jaded connoisseurs, awed by its beauty and precision.

And by the way, I still have the carved, deep blue lapis horse that Captain Afonivich gave me as a birthday present. It stands within easy reach on a table next to the malachite box studded with amber, a gift from Zulu, engraved with these words: GOOD FRIENDS SHALL MEET ONCE MORE.

In the mysterious world of intelligence, this token gesture might confuse some people. But Zulu's reason for giving me that box had to do with the fact that he respected the nobility of my conviction.

People from all walks of life flocked to Pomme d'Or. Some came to be seen, to gossip, to shop; others came to drink tea from the silver samovar that had once belonged to the exquisite ballerina, Malthilde Kachessinska, the mistress of Tsar Nicholas before he ascended the centuries-old Romanov throne.

Another interesting habitué of the shop was a handsome dandy with slicked-down hair, clean-shaven, dressed with elegance in fine tailor-made suits, (undoubtedly Savile Row) who came daily to Pomme d'Or at the stroke of two. Ordinarily, he came alone, although sometimes one plainclothes policeman sat on a chair, eyes glued on him. This character spoke French with a curious accent and the serene aloofness of his eyes shadowed with long lashes were a joy to behold.

The high point of each day was this man's arrival. He turned his attention almost immediately to the tiny pianos. And at each visit he bought one. It was bizarre, but I kept my mouth shut, for I didn't want to scare away a good customer, such as he was. Besides, he was a feast to the eyes, which was not surprising since only a few men are chiseled with such gusto.

One day in early spring, when you fancy you can smell lilacs, the man arrived holding a huge bunch of white and purple lilacs scented as the ones in my imagination. The stunning flowers he presented to me gave me enough courage to ask him just what he did with all those pianos. He smiled but said nothing. I felt my face turning red and my ears were burning as if someone had lit a match to them. I was sure I had crossed the boundaries of the clerk and customer relationship. Just when I was silently reproaching myself for my faux-pas, suddenly the man metamorphosed from a moth into a lively silkworm that actually could talk.

"Mademoiselle, so you find my passion for the piano a little on the strange side. I can understand that," he said with a faraway look, as if searching through the dossier of his memory.

"Hmmm . . . maybe a little," I answered, cautiously.

"Well, isn't that interesting. But before you jump to any conclusion of your own, let me explain. My childhood was restrictive and unhappy. I, at least, was able to find an absorbing interest of my own. It took the sting out of my despair. I began collecting small woodwind instruments. Soon after, I started to also collect pianos. Pianos are my passion, now."

"To be honest, I myself am not into collecting things in large numbers. But, I do respect others' need for collecting."

"I'm not your typical collector. I collect only things that speak to me."

"I can understand that. By the way, are you a musician? You have that certain aura that sets you apart from the ordinary mortals."

"I hate to disappoint you, but I'm not a musician. I just like to play the piano. My dream is, however, someday to become a concert pianist."

"Well . . . what's stopping you? Is it money? If you are short of funds, perhaps I can help you. Life is too short for putting one's dream on the back burner, don't you agree?"

"It is very gallant of you indeed. You are very kind. In fact, it's the nicest thing anyone ever told me. Thank you for your support."

"Sure, anytime. The piano . . . when did it become your passion?"

"To answer that correctly, I have to go back to my childhood—when I was a mere boy of six—to the exact moment when my father gave me a piano, and I was smitten almost instantly. With the piano came a terrific teacher, Monsieur van der Zelt, a blind man, who came daily to the palace."

"Excuse me, did you say palace? What palace are we talking here?"

"Hmm . . . do you mind if I don't elaborate?"

"Sure. I respect your need for privacy. By the way, I am Summer Grant from San Francisco, California."

"I am delighted to meet you. I am . . . Prince Osman, the son of Sultan Abdul Hamid," he whispered ever so quietly as if there were flying moths in the room—fitted with hidden listening devices.

"*Enchanté* Prince Osman. I am, indeed, honored to make your most charming acquaintance."

"Please call me Salih Demirel, a fictitious name that allows me to travel incognito."

"Don't worry. Your secret is safe with me."

"Thank you, Mademoiselle Grant. I rarely, and only when it is absolutely necessary, talk to strangers. But, you were so easy to trust. In this case, maybe it was the look in your kind eyes—which are simply bewitching—or maybe it was your velvety voice, or the way you pronounced my name, or . . . but I think it was your body language that told me you can be trusted."

"You flatter me, thank you," I said, feeling like a proud peacock with a magnificent plumage.

"I am serious. I meant every word."

"Thank you again. I wish my mother could be here to meet you. She adores men with history."

"Perhaps some day I shall have the pleasure of meeting her."

"She would like that."

"Before I say *adieu*, let me say just how much I enjoyed our little chat. I look forward to seeing you again."

"Yes, I know. Tomorrow two o'clock on the button."

"Your sense of humor is refreshing. I like that."

"Till then, I'll try to keep the clock running."

"*Adieu*, Summer," Salih said and shook my hand,

bowing respectfully. "I hope you will allow me the pleasure of dining with you."

"Sure. Why not? I would like that. Thank you."

Even now, as it was then, I can't explain the magnetism of this perfect stranger, who still makes me feel like an errant balloon wandering in the sky. What I never anticipated, nor for that matter, did anyone else—was that I would eventually fall in love with Salih and lose him to an assassin's bullet—all in the same year. But, for now, I was happy to be riding uncharted waters close to shore.

Every year, autumn arrives in Constantinople in a mass of color—creating a riotous chiaroscuro on the shores of the Marmara Sea. That year was no exception. The days, as they've done for many years, alternated between sunny, warm and cool with salty breezes. In some part of my head I was aware I hadn't seen or heard from Salih for quite awhile. I was worried. Then at the end of October I came across an article in *Hurriet* that explained it all.

Mustafa Kemal, who in a different time might have been an Alexander the Great, or a Genghis Khan, was now the most powerful man in Turkey, in absolute control of the country. This was the dawn of a new Turkey that had abolished the Sultanate, deported Salih's father, Abdul Hamid, his three wives, two sons, several concubines, eunuchs and servants—to live comfortably in a villa in Salonika, and had banished Mohamet V, the last Sultan, to San Remo, Italy, and bundled off Abdul Mejid, Calif of all Faithful, a man unversed in the ways of the world, to Switzerland, to live among the civilized Swiss, who welcomed him.

Turkey was now an independent republic. Its leader

was known as Kemal Ataturk—Kemal meaning strong and Ataturk meaning the father of Turks.

Then, one cold day in November, despite the wind's drama in the skeletal trees outside the windows, Salih arrived at Pomme d'Or unsmiling and as pale as a ghost fresh out of the grave. He was clutching a small bunch of violets in one hand and a book in the other.

"Summer, I have missed you. You've got to believe that. In my imagination I have strewn every street that you walked with scented roses. I wanted desperately to see you, but I was told to avoid the masses and all major throughways in the city, because of an intercepted communication by a Turkish intelligence officer that talked about a planned attack by an organized crime mob called 'The Armenian Arm.' I don't know whether you know that there is a growing awareness among the Turks that the Armenians will not rest until they annihilate all those who spat upon them, while killing fifty-five thousand men—just in the village of Arkanz in Asia Minor. Their pain is real, and so is mine."

"Salih, I'm really sorry. Is there anything I can do?"

"Just be my friend," Salih said and handed me the flowers and book. "Just like Marcel Proust, I am also a *la recherché du temps perdu*. I'm off to Paris to study music at the great Paris Conservatoire. I want the world to remember me as an accomplished pianist, rather than the son of an Ottoman Sultan with two hundred concubines, who was hated by so many," Salih continued, blowing cigarette smoke into the air in small circles.

"Thank you for the violets—my all time favorite flower, and the book. I've been a Proust fan since reading about the madeleines slowly disintegrating in the coffee while he ponders about life. Thank you. You are such a dear."

"Yes, I suppose I am."

"I shall miss your daily visits. On the other hand, I'm happy that you are finally going to realize your dream. I'm indeed proud to have known you," I said gingerly, yet feeling as sad as an orphaned cub left alone in a forest.

"Maybe I'm a fool to chase such a magnificent obsession, but . . . even fools must now and then be right," Salih said with a shy little smile.

I heard the voice of my conscience urging me to hold and console Salih. But before I could take a step or utter a few comforting words, he hurried out of the store and into a waiting car, hoping the tears would go unnoticed.

I watched with great sadness as the car moved forward toward the tunnel and disappeared down the steep hill to Galata Bridge.

4

There are voices which we hear in solitude, but they
grow faint and inaudible as we enter the world.
                                                    —Ralph Waldo Emerson

Legend among the locals has it that if summer begins
with an explosion of sunshine, there will be a trembling
on the surface of the moon.

Who would have guessed that in the second week of
July, as if by magic, white-draped tables gleaming with
crystal and silver would sprout in the gardens of Mon
Plaisir, to celebrate the legend and sort out truth from
error?

Another fascinating feature of the party was the
group of superbly dressed women, who came ablaze with
jewels chosen from their own personal stash. It was
impossible to tell where one of them began and the other
ended.

Reading through my journals of this period so many
years later brings back memories of the music, alternat-
ing between slow and fast in an atmosphere of champagne, cigarettes and perfume, played by a band
hovering on the Bohemian fringes. The musicians were
totally absorbed in themselves, as if driven by a curious
sense of some destiny.

By eleven o'clock when the blossoms were fast asleep
and young lovers had retreated to quiet corners, there
were still a great many dancers who continued to ebb and

42

flow onto the glass dance floor, indifferent to others' existence and oblivious of the sleeping birds in the trees and of the exotic fishes beneath their feet, doing their own version of the Charleston as erotically as fish can do. Sometime after midnight when the chatter rose a notch above crescendo, and champagne had taken hold of my senses, I left the eccentrically dressed guests, who were chatting and dancing and chatting yet again, to sit by myself in the rose garden next to the sea, yet high enough to escape the spray of saltwater. With such a dramatic change in scenery, from the glamorous to the peaceful, I decided to take a quick dip. As I was about to step out of my dress, I heard a strange rustling in the bushes at the bottom of the rose garden. But I was too intoxicated to care about anything, including Amelia's ghost, who often haunted the beach, covered in seaweed. She was no threat to me. I had grown to like her, despite her garish attires that were nothing short of absurd.

Had I been sober, common sense would have prevailed. But as my passion for the sea swelled up inside me, I readied myself to dive into the water. I recall leaning against the iron railing and imagining a sea nymph coming out from the depths of the sea, waving her hands and motioning me to join her. Shortly afterward, two arms grabbed me and held me tight, and a warm hand grazed my breasts. Wow! My first thought was Amelia, for often she tapped my shoulder or pulled my hair just to let me know she was present. But, I assure you, the hand that touched me was a far cry from one of Amelia's icy paws. Now, paralyzed with fright, I wondered whose arms were holding me so firmly, yet so gently. Then in a moonbeam I saw the face and smelled the breath exuding a strong smell of alcohol. Terror fell upon me like a thunderclap. Uncle Hugh's eyes were consuming me with a strange glow. I remember seeing a similar glow in the eyes of a black panther eyeing the people who were watching him from behind the fence at the San Francisco zoo.

I freed myself from the clasp of Uncle Hugh's arms. I literally flew from the garden to the safety of my room and locked the door. I was out of breath and trembling like a leaf in the wind. I stared at my own reflection staring back at me in the mirror. *Aaque!* My face had taken on a waxy look, my lips were cold and my eyes expressed horror. With my ghostly appearance I could easily be a stand-in for Amelia. I turned away from the hideous sight and buried my face in the sleeve of my kimono.

The following night was made for poets; the moonlight danced on the water, the nightingales sang in the trees, and a breeze heavy with the scents of roses, lilacs and lavender carried their fragrances to me. Perhaps, it was these interlocking wonders without beginning or ending, that inspired me to make love to Uncle Hugh— absente reo—while we listened to "Amour c'est un oiseau" from Bizet's *Carmen*. This combination of lust and music was an irresistible force that transformed me into a fiery Carmen singing with Don José—*C'est toi! C'est moi!*

It is amazing that I would do such a foolish thing. I must have been moonstruck or I must plead temporary insanity. Yet, the other me, who got me into all sorts of trouble, had a wonderful time! Making such a shameless admission isn't something most people are willing to do. Funny, isn't it, how one passionate embrace that beckons the flesh makes you a believer in the ways of sin, regardless of your sense of right or wrong.

At that point of my personal sexual revolution, I wish I knew what was going through my mind.

That year winter arrived in a snowy fury. Mon Plaisir, always lovely in any season, became a veritable fairyland with sparkling icicles and drifts of snow. Early in December, Uncle Hugh left for Brussels to champion for a humanitarian cause dear to his heart. These short trips usually ended up in famous chocolate shops, which gave me something to look forward to. Uncle Hugh promised to be back before Christmas, now only two weeks away.

With Uncle Hugh gone and Boris, the valet, busy preparing himself to play Santa Claus to the émigré community, and the fact that I was putting in long hours at the Pomme d'Or—due to a hectic late November and early December—it was a miracle that I found a Christmas tree in Pera. The tree wasn't anything to brag about. In fact, it was plain ugly. But its spirit spoke to me.

I decorated the tree with every shiny ornament available in town. Some had been made in Constantinople at the turn of the century, and others that I found in the shop of Frau Lippe were made in Germany. The ones made in Constantinople were made mostly of embossed cardboard painted on both sides. But the stars of my collection were the German ornaments—in the most extraordinary shapes; Santas, angels, vegetables, fruits, icicles and gilded walnuts.

Despite my busy schedule, my shopping sprees and the endless yule parties, this period of loneliness was the winter of my discontent. I missed Uncle Hugh frightfully. Feeling cheerless, I tented myself with an abyssal melancholy, which kept me in the nostalgic clutches of Christmases gone by.

Throughout my childhood, the only constant had been holidays spent at the Red Poppy, our winery nestled in the hills of the historic Sonoma Valley, California. Red

Poppy was an 800-acre parcel, a delightful Valhalla where we were allowed to be children with mud up to our eyeballs. Going to the Red Poppy for Christmas was a tradition handed down for generations of Daudets—starting with Grandpapa Marcel, my maternal grandfather, who was an expert vineyard keeper, born into a world of extraordinary privilege and who was said to be diligent, headstrong and a mean flute player.

At the southern end of the Red Poppy, hidden under a canopy of rampant honeysuckle, was Le Petit Chateau. It was the fantasy of my grandpapa, who wanted a Burgundian winery in the heart of California's wine oenophile country. We used it for our home.

Each Christmas at Le Petit Chateau we decorated two trees: the Senior Folly and the Junior Folly. The Senior Folly was a giant noble pine with wide-spreading branches. The branches, like the wings of a giant prehistoric bird, were adorned with antique ornaments, sharing space with beautiful glass ropes and hundreds of small colored candles. If this sounds too spectacular, it's because it was.

On the other hand, the Junior Folly was a much smaller tree, which can best be described as a rhapsody in living color. It was decorated with objects only children can imagine and love—barnyard animals, birds, balloons, red sleighs, golden apples and pears with faces, and Santas in varied crimson clothes. To be honest, I have never seen such a fanciful tree since. Perhaps I stopped searching, because of loyalty being stronger than vanity.

Some holidays are shaped by simple pleasures—like the Noels at Le Petit Chateau. On Christmas morning, one could almost taste, feel and smell the energy running all throughout the house with an electrifying speed. Among the earliest clippings in my scrapbook is a picture titled: "The heavenly Christmas of the celebrated Grants." To this day, I treasure it.

After opening presents with the adults, we could hardly wait to join our own tree waiting for us in the children's wing.

I will never forget those moments of exquisite ecstasy when we pulled down nougats, wrapped in bright cellophane, marzipan fruits with eyes and ears, tiny crystallized orange and apricot pieces, chocolate in every imaginable shape and size, all screaming in unison, open me first, eat me first, yes me . . . yes me . . .

We even had entertainment provided by mechanical monkeys beating on drums, tall giraffes running among dancing bears and spotted cats and tawny lions that did not quite fit.

All this was a long, long time ago. Yet it feels as if we were children with stars in our eyes . . . only yesterday. To this day, it thrills me to describe in detail our family Christmases in California.

5

No man is a hypocrite in his pleasures.
                                    —Samuel Johnson

Being primarily a sensuous woman, I put much romantic nonsense into my fantasies—like the time when I was foolish enough to believe that someday, if and when the occasion arose, Uncle Hugh would be my legendary deflorationist—more handsome, more magical, more incredible than any other man on earth. This, of course, was a wish in a private dream with a fairy tale ending. Yet, despite my fascination with lust, I wondered if, in reality, sexual intercourse was everything that it was cracked up to be.

You see, no matter how many times you have lusted for sex in your imagination, fantasy never lives up to its full potential as opposed to reality. Tired of imaginary sexual gratifications that never amounted to anything, I was determined to find out the true meaning of sex. And to rise to the occasion, I chose Christmas Eve 1927 as the target date. As I said, I was curious and anxious. That erotic interest was like tapping on a hive to excite the bees. Now, there was no turning back. I had to go through with it.

In my day, unlike it is now, schools didn't offer sexual education classes. One had to find one's way in the dark. Sex appeal—in the true meaning of the word—was an erotic charm that you either had, or you created with the help of a special perfume made from the foreskin secretion of the male beaver (for which the North American Indians were famous).

December 24 was drawing to a close when Boris brought into the drawing room a tray with a bottle of rare champagne that he had discovered at a certain French *Charcuterie et Marchant des Liqueurs Spiritueuses* nestled between the colorful and scented flower stands in the Flower Passage, off Grande Rue de Pera. I believed him when he remarked, "*Mon Dieu!* Trying to find that champagne in Pera was like looking for a needle in a haystack."

Anyway, we had champagne, snowflakes dancing against the window panes, shadowy images on the Christmas tree, flames pirouetting in the fireplace and fantastic champagne bubbles in our heads—all things magical that contributed to my victory. And . . . there was a pair of sea-green eyes that were reaching to the depths of my soul, breaking all reserves of restraint. I don't remember whether or not the eyes were a part of my well-orchestrated scheme, but if they were, they surely added to the pleasure—already way beyond my expectation.

I cannot honestly tell you when and how it all started, because the events of that night are a bit hazy, like the remains of a dream in the mind. By some miracle and the help of my imagination, I believe it was about the time when I saw myself as Anna Karenina in the arms of Vronsky in full-dress white uniform with gold aiguillettes—at one of the "Bals Roses" given by the St. Petersburg high society.

Now, as I look back to the epoch of my inner revolution with more mature eyes, I grow uncomfortable, yet I understand why the real me gave in to the other me who, at that point in time, craved affection and wanted to shed her virginity.

Thus, I didn't argue with my conscience whether it was right or wrong to abandon myself to my desires, and let Uncle Hugh deflower me. What good would that have accomplished? The way I saw it, the decision was already made by my destiny. Now I was just a simple vehicle to carry out this segment of the master plan.

I'm sure Uncle Hugh thought he was being nice when he took me into his arms, caressing and kissing me gently. After all it was Christmas Eve, a time for love. As for me, I knew deep in my heart that what I was about to do was taboo. Yet, I responded to his kisses with all the fire of hell. He pushed me away, but I continued to press myself against his body, nuzzling his ears and neck like a silkworm nibbling on mulberry leaves. Suddenly, to my great delight, Uncle Hugh lost his composure that had been, until now, in perfect check. I shall never forget the moment when he unfastened the teeny-weeny buttons of my red cashmere sweater and my breasts slipped freely into his eager hands. The warmth of his tongue tracing my nipples—now growing hard—aroused in me strange sensations I had never felt before, for he was the first man ever to put his lips on my fully developed breasts. Suddenly, I was no longer Summer Grant, the apple of my father's eye. In a heartbeat I had metamorphosed into a beautiful Juliet and Uncle Hugh my handsome Romeo. The untold truth, however, was that I was a romantic caught in a Victorian body who, until now, had looked at the world through a prism with a phallus.

In the middle of the fabulous dream in progress, my imagination kicked in, my defense mechanism shut down and my fears of The Thing, and my qualms about the actual sexual act whooshed by in a blur. My body quivered in a narcissistic spasm that sent electrifying impulses to every corner of my already feverish body. At that moment of sexual desire, to incite abstinence was akin to asking Satan to take Holy Communion.

By stretching of the imagination one can only guess what my uncle's thoughts were when he stood up to take off his gray wool pants—exposing a part of the male anatomy I had never seen before.

Wonder of wonders, I gasped as I laid my eyes on *le grand chose;* the unknown male organ that had haunted me all my life with a certain amount of curiosity and fear. At long last, the naked truth stood in front of me in the whole panoply of lust and desire. *The thing* wasn't nearly as scary as I was led to believe. In fact, the forbidden fruit was rather funny-looking, a ripply body crowned with a purplish halo. It was so comical, I had to laugh.

The details of what followed are lost in the mists of time. However, I have a memory of us stretched out in front of a mirror, watching the writhing movement of our bodies on the silk damask sofa—as *the thing* teased my secret part with small playful thrusts that flamed the fires within.

Then the inevitable happened, like a clap of thunder. A sudden prickly sensation, almost a burning pain, ripped me open. I could feel *the thing* gliding into my vagina, piercing the last barrier of my chastity with the accuracy of a pistol. I let out a muffled cry and grimaced like an angry baboon in a zoo. Uncle Hugh, upon hearing my groan and seeing the trace of distress on my face, drew *the thing* out, but continued to move it back and forth, until he was sure my desire matched his. Then in a moment of exquisite pain he gave a furious thrust and I heard angels sing. At that moment of sexual ecstasy I felt like a star blowing its outer atmosphere into space in billowing clouds of gas.

In the course of the winter night the falling snow had

transformed the village into an enchanted fairyland with thick layers of glistening white mass; the sky was one gray flush; the sea gleamed like polished hematite; the room echoed with the sound of popping wood. This scene, as lovely as a haunting tune, had changed nothing. Mon Plaisir still led a life all of its own. The tall minarets still clamped together the rugged edges of earth and sky. Uncle Hugh was still Uncle Hugh. Obviously, I was the only one that had changed. I was no longer a virgin. That part of my life was gone, gone with the wind. Vanished.

6

Hell is paved with good intentions.
                              —Samuel Johnson

One wintry day in January, when a blizzard had transformed the Seven Hills of Constantinople into seven daz-
zling brides, I awoke with a warm blanket to my belly and
one heavy bundle at my back. The memory of incest, in
which I initiated Uncle Hugh into the game of sin, was
now the hateful present that robbed me of happiness and
held me captive with thoughts of hell. It was a subject on
which I ruminated a good deal, because I had sinned
against God's Ten Commandments: not to give way to
lust.

That same day, as darkness fell on the same Seven
Hills, now shrouded with snow and ice, Boris delivered to
the Swallow's Nest a purple-edged envelope scented with
lavender; Uncle Hugh's favorite cologne since his boulevardier days in Paris. With a fast beating heart, I opened
the envelope and read it by the light of the moon reflected
from the sea. Each line was larded with a certain amount
of tristesse, which made me think I had fallen into a
world of silent ghosts and funeral wreaths tied with purple bows.

I cannot explain nor interpret the meaning of the following poem. But, I believe it was written in a mood of
agonized anxiety.

Sombre come la nuit, je n'ai pas d'esperance,
Moi seul ne connait pas de plaisir enchante.
Ah, quand un rêve d'or adoucit ma souffrance
Pourquoi reparais-tu, triste realité?

One might ask, why this poem and why now? Well, let me say that among Uncle Hugh's many passions was poetry. He used poetry as a vehicle to express whatever was in his heart and soul. His life was such that he had no reason to invent drama, yet it was through poetry that he was able to satisfy his insatiable craving for it.

Forty years have gone by. I became an author. I married and had wonderful memories. But it is only now, after many moons that I come to realize just how important those poems were to Uncle Hugh.

Come to think of it, George Bizet said it with music, so did Chopin and Tchaikovsky. Lord Byron said it with poems, as did Emerson and Browning. So...why not Uncle Hugh? The only difference, however, was that Uncle Hugh almost always wrote in French—a language that he adored and considered to be a civilized tongue for expressing one's passion.

Meanwhile, I tried to imitate the way Uncle Hugh wrote. But it was no use. He had a way with poetry, and I took refuge in writing my novels. Many years later, I found a copy of an old poem tucked in one of my books. It was like running into an old friend. The poem told me once again that Uncle Hugh loved me way before I knew what love was all about.

Je Veux ton Coeur!
Vien! La premiere rose est nee
C'est le signale des jours heureux!
Vien! Tout fleurie sous la feuillee,

La brise est douce et perfume,
La val est vert, le bois ombreux!
Je veux ton coeur, o jeune fille!
Ta douce voix chère a l'echo!

The freezing temperatures of that severe winter almost destroyed all the flowers in San Stefano. Despite the weather's bravado, the new year moved on a hopeful note. The previous years had seen many mega reforms in Turkey, as Ataturk struggled to create a modern nation. After abolishing the harem and the polygamy, he did away with the veil, the fez and the Ottoman titles. Ultimately he introduced the Latin alphabet and coeducational classes. Some of those changes created feelings of alarm such as the Turks had never known.

However, while the country plied Ataturk with honors, the tragic death of the ill-fated Fikriye—probably the only woman who truly loved Ataturk—went almost unnoticed, in spite of the fact that her body was found in an alley with a bullet through the heart.

Through all that, Constantinople's spirit remained a curious mixture of yesterday, today, and tomorrow. Now in every park, café, school and home a new breed of Turks asked themselves about the rumored atrocities against the Armenians in Anatolya and the Greeks in Smyrna. The curious minds wanted to know whether these were fabricated lies to divide the Muslims from the Christians, or were they exaggerated facts blended skillfully with fiction?

Whatever one's views were, the Turks really loved Ataturk.

Yet, many progressive university students questioned the reports presented to them. Their minds were preoccupied with the growing rumors that thousands of

Armenians—from Van and all the way to Baghdad line—were robbed, beaten, raped and murdered by the Turks, Arabs, Kurds, as they made their way across the arid Syrian desert. Some of these atrocities were captured on celluloid; others etched in memory permanently.

And there was the matter of Smyrna, a heavenly seaport on the Aegean Sea, for centuries the cradle of Greek legends that had inspired Homer to write his Odyssey. The fires of Smyrna and the stench of burning flesh were issues that haunted every Turk, Greek, Armenian and Jew.

As the balmy days of spring approached the hot days of summer, two things captivated my attention: the beauty of my roses and the euphoria of intelligence. They were different; but together, no matter how seemingly far apart, they added new levels of passion. The insouciant flowers provided me with lyrical moments amid the parterres of roses that were brought to San Stefano from all corners of the world. Roses delighted me as much as they must have pleased Sappho, who in 600 B.C. named the rose the Queen of Flowers and, according to a legend, Cupid presented a rose to Harpocrates, the God of Silence, to ensure that the affair of Venus, his mother, would remain a well-hidden secret.

I will go ahead and shatter a few illusions by saying that the thrill of espionage is as gratifying as the beauty of a rose, or a haunting melody. Because the thrill of gathering secret information in the most unlikely places pumps you with adrenaline in a mega way. Strange bedfellows—rose and spy.

Often when the weather blessed us with idyllic conditions favorable for strolling, Uncle Hugh and I tippytoed on scented clouds in a garden of white roses—as penned by Guillaume de Lorris in the thirteenth century *lai.* From our perch we watched the dance of the butter-flies. As they fluttered on hundreds of flowers, they created a ballet of such beauty, only surpassed by Nijinsky's leap which made ballet history, I wrote in my memoirs.

Now I'm a woman with loose skin above the eyelids and a mouth festooned with wrinkles. But my memory still regales me with past treasures, like the time when Uncle Hugh and I half-buried ourselves in the warm, damp sand and made love with such passion it felt as if we rose in the air and floated over the sea. This passionate act gave sex a new style, as beautiful as the words of Sir Walter Scott:

> Like the dew on the mountains,
> Like the foam on the river,
> Like the bubble on the fountain.

I would be lying if I told you that my diary does not abound with similar experiences—because it does. And I can say quite frankly that nothing on earth ever surpassed those moments of sheer rapture by the sea—when in a moment of great passion—Uncle Hugh and I, in the closest of all embraces with skins touching—stopped being ourselves and became Apollo and Aphrodite lost somewhere in Greek mythology, like two desperadoes searching for cover.

Just when I thought I had my destiny by the tail, and not sure how I had managed it, fate threw me a curve by adding impending motherhood to my repertoire of pleasures. A fact that the local sophisticates were quick to notice.

I remember the idle talk circulating in and out of the gossip hotbeds of the American colony in Constantinople. Their attitude toward my relationship with Uncle Hugh was puzzling. They spoke openly about it and looked anxiously to reveal an ugly underbelly to something that was sensuously beautiful, but otherwise unconventional. "Can a woman take fire to her bosom and expect her clothes not to burn?" they said loud enough to make people shake their heads in utter disgust. *"Une affaire scandaleuse!"* they repeated as they continued to target our illegitimate relationship with their poison darts. To their way of thinking our strange union of two opposites was like exchanging a mule for a horse to gallop down a crooked path. This was somewhat of a surprise, for many of them were as guilty as I when it came to affairs of the heart. Regardless of the ongoing gossip, I was beside myself that a baby was on its way to complete my life.

Soon, the innuendoes that had continued for several weeks settled down, and my life returned to normalcy, but with a slight difference. Now there were shopping trips to the Layetterie Parisienne where I purchased clothes, bedding, toys, pictures and accessories. I worried constantly about the baby's comfort and its health. Hardly a day went by when I didn't talk, sing, or tap little messages with my fingers to the life growing within me. It was all so new, so exciting.

Yes, yes, yes, this had to be the summer of my happiness.

Meanwhile, Uncle Hugh and I braced ourselves for the vitriol that would be unleashed by the Grants in San Francisco.

When the news of my pregnancy reached the shores of San Francisco, it caused a stink more powerful than a skunk's. I, the apple of my daddy's eye, had brought shame on the family that wanted me to be the living display of their virtue—whatever that meant. With a few bitter words, Daddy made sure I understood that the jewel of the Grant dynasty was dead. *Morte. Finie. Abiit cum vento!* In other words: my father simply couldn't forgive my less than virtuous lifestyle. Strangely enough, there was not a word said about Uncle Hugh. It was as if I had made this baby all by myself, and Uncle Hugh had nothing to do with the condition I was in. I wondered why my father was protecting him, while throwing me to the wolves? Surely Daddy was smart enough to know that babies simply didn't happen all by themselves; this wasn't an "Immaculate Conception." That controversial theory belonged to the "Virgin Mary," the mother of Jesus, whose pregnancy was announced by an angel, while I was merely an earthling.

To start off, let me tell you that the Grants—one of the most respected families in San Francisco—had a double standard all their own. And they were smug with that. They knew who they were and where they had come from. It was into this aristocratic arrogance of "We are okay, but not you" climate that my father, christened Jack Andrew, was born in 1882. He was a handsome baby with rosy cheeks and a killer smile that gave one the impression that he was destined for leadership. The Grants were very proud to be the parents of such a lovely specimen whom they displayed with great care, as though he were a precious object that could break easily.

The entire Grant clan obeyed religiously all the laws of their faith—Roman Catholic—at least on the surface. Ironically enough, they resented any challenges to their deeply rooted religious tenets; albeit rife with personal exceptions on their behalf. To my young self, this was a charade meant for the simpletons at large.

Anyway, the details of what followed have never been too clear in my memory. Because on that particular day, my head was full of strange noises as though hundreds of incarcerated bugs were digging their way out from hidden prisons somewhere in my brain. Perhaps... maybe...what I was hearing was my baby's struggle through the birth canal, to reach freedom. It was about that time when I experienced my first contraction. I was in my eighth month and had felt great until now. The sheer thought of an early delivery was enough to send Uncle Hugh into a tailspin. Within minutes we were in a car with only a small suitcase, driving to the American Hospital located in the upper reaches of Pera.

Late afternoon of the same bittersweet day, by a cruel stroke of luck, I gave birth to a stillborn baby, a girl. She was a very small person who, even in death, had a certain aloofness not usually associated with the newly born. This tiniest of all angels, who never had a chance to sprout her own wings, weighed four pounds and was twenty inches long. Her dimpled pink cheeks resembled a half-opened bud. The perfection of her body was bound to be a prototype for other gods to imitate. Choirs of angels must have sung as God blew life into her, for He knew He had outdone Himself. Also, equally—and perhaps even more beautiful were her creamy skin and her mass of golden hair, reasons enough for God to call her back.

As I struggled with my emotions, once again the Bible became a source of comfort and inspiration. Because this was a death that I could neither understand nor accept.

In the meantime, my life was in shambles. Now that my baby was dead, it was only a matter of time for the final send-off. On that day, as I listened to the church bell echoing through the pines and the magnolias, I fantasized about life in Heaven. By far this wasn't an ordinary day in San Stefano. The tolling bell was announcing the death of a child; dead long before its time.

A Requiem was held at the local Catholic Church, St. Mary. Halfway through the service, I became aware that I wasn't the only one crying. There were tears in St. Therese's marble eyes. Then I saw a bright and a beautiful light filling the space between us. This was an amazing sight. Then . . . in the blink of an eye, I saw my baby lying peacefully in the arms of an angel with white wings. Together they were traveling through the light. I assumed the angel was taking my baby to Heaven, because God needed a very special rose in His garden. But what about the scent of roses that clung to my clothing after they were gone?

Strangely enough, during those puzzling moments, I thought if my baby were alive, she might have raised a big fuss over the censer pouring forth a cloud of grayish smoke, thick enough to choke a pony.

On that day, it seemed as though the whole village had staggered forth to be with my baby. I had never thought it was possible for an entire village to love a baby so deeply to my great astonishment.

They carried bunches of flowers, mostly tulips. I was not sure why all those tulips. Later, I was told each tulip represented the soul of a departed one.

When the cortege reached the Holy Ghost Cemetery, nestled in a small park of blooming Judah trees, I wondered about the cloud of black and yellow butterflies escorting the coffin. Suddenly they disappeared, only to appear again when the coffin was laid beside the yawning abyss. In my memoirs of the day I wrote: As I entered the cemetery, I felt like a shapeless shadow draped in severe black. The entire face of the silent park was honeycombed with flowers—wild peonies, tulips, primroses and Madonna lilies—which gave the illusion that this was a friendly region. Despite the show of color, I believe a cemetery is a mysterious place where the dead go to embrace death in order to obtain eternal life.

I sobbed softly under my black veil, for everything seemed beyond my control. I felt a sharp pain in my chest that spread across my shoulders and arms. I was sure I was about to have a heart attack. I reached for Uncle Hugh's arm to steady myself and bring some sort of calm to my racing heart. Despite my extreme agony, I was determined to give a royal send-off to the small body that was turning to dust right before our eyes.

"Good-bye . . . my sweet little angel. Though I never had a chance to suckle you at my breast, you will always be with me. That's a promise that I intend to keep forever," I whispered and flung myself at the coffin, and fell into the hole. I was so shaken by the experience, I burst into tears. With tears streaming down my face, I grabbed the coffin and kissed my baby one last time.

Words . . . I don't think there are enough words in any dictionary to express correctly the suffering of any mother who loses a child to death. Surely, I'm not alone in feeling this way.

As I thought deeply about all this, I told myself that someday when I was much older, perhaps then death and I could become roommates. Until then it wouldn't be necessary for me to be friends with the angel of death. God would have to take care of the rest.

7

There is only one success—to be able to spend
your life in your own way.
　　　　　　　　　　—Christopher Morley

If I remember rightly, it was during Ramadan, which fell
in the Ides of March that year, when a chance encounter
brought back a part of me that I had left in San Francisco.

As a teenager on the cusp of adulthood, I manifested
a taste for myths and legends. That, I suppose, marked
the beginning of my interest in folklore. From simple
fairy tales, I moved on and began documenting unusual
anecdotes for future reference, hoping someday to write a
book on folklore.

Thus, can you imagine my joy that day on the train
when my seatmate, who sat knitting feverishly a sweater
of some sort, asked me quite unexpectedly if I was familiar with the legend of "The Lost Souls?"

"No," I replied, "but I'd love to hear all about it."

"Well, now, aren't you lucky? I'm a renowned collector
of ancient Turkish legends, and there is nothing I would
rather do than talk about them."

"Indeed, lucky. I better knock on wood."

"I should say so. You don't want to tempt the devil—
do you, now? As far as legends go, the top legend of the
Istanbulus these days is the one of the Lost Souls, which
is a story like no other—about a particular species of
tubenose sea birds. However, through the years, the leg-

end has given these shear birds the souls of hundreds of harem women, who were thrown into the sea to drown. There is more to this tale, but unfortunately I have to get off at the next stop—Bakirkoy. My! How time flies! How delightful to talk to someone with similar interests. On the other hand, why not go and see the birds yourself?" she said with ease, the culture barrier overcome by her knowledge of a few English words and her ability with the sign language.

"What a great idea. I should have thought of it myself. Because I've always had an enormous passion for legends," I replied without skipping a beat.

"Well . . . *Allahaismarladik*, good-bye. If you ever come to Bakirkoy, please look me up. I live near the park in an old wooden Victorian. Here is my name and address," the lady said and handed me a small card with the information.

"*Inshallah!*—God willing," I answered and shook her hand.

As I recall it was on one of those hot August days—when heat shafts visibly dance on ancient land walls and when only a lizard darts out from under cool stones—my camera slinging from my neck and toting a briefcase, I flew on wings of hope in search of the alleged black birds, (a.k.a. lost souls), who were still haunting the waters of the Bosphorus.

Sure enough, the sea and the horizon were there, but the birds were nowhere to be seen.

Disappointed, but not discouraged, I approached an old man who seemed to be half-asleep under the shade of a large fig tree, in the passive loneliness of the years, his watery eyes lost in some private memory. I made little noises, just loud enough to make him aware of my presence. He opened his eyes slowly and gazed at me in total wonder as if I were a fig that had just fallen off the tree.

"Hanim . . . what are you doing here? Are you lost? Are you looking for someone or something—like a glass of cool water?" he asked, bringing his eyes into focus.

"Well . . . in a way, I am. I'm looking for the Lost Souls. As they say in fairy tales, black birds with human souls. Perhaps you know something about them and you can tell me if I'm anywhere close to the area where they hang out?"

"Here, have a fresh fig, miss," the old man said and handed me a giant black fig. "Unlike other Bosphorus birds, these black birds fly in groups and are easy to spot when they are out there. As for you, just keep walking. Keep your eyes focused. Because sooner or later you'll find them."

"Thank you for your encouraging words. Good-bye."

"Good luck, miss."

I continued my search treading along tortuous sunken alleys, filled with the detritus of the ages. At one point I almost stepped on a rotting cat, lying beside a dog's carcass that lay next to an iron pot, cascading with mint and red geranium. Despite the state of the neighborhood, I felt quite at home, as though I had lived here in a previous incarnation.

A mile or so further west, at a point close to shore, I saw shadows rippling in the water. They were gliding, plunging, and soaring through the air on blade-like wings. My eyes filled with fascination at the turn of every wing. "I made it! By God, I made it!" I yelled into the summer sky, now sure that what I was seeing were, indeed, the Lost Souls. This was a triumph over a doubtful outcome.

Before the day was over, I noted in my journal the following entry: Today I found the fabled birds. It was a magnificent sight. I followed them with my eyes, as they skimmed the surface of the water at a mile a minute, their dark plumes merging with the deep-blue waters of the Bosphorus. I believe they were the souls of the unwanted women, who were tied in heavy sacks and left to drown in the currents of the sea. This explanation is simple. However, I feel that there is more to this story than what meets the eye. I intend to pursue it.

Now loaded with a new supply of adrenaline and bent on learning the truth about the birds—like so many writers before me, I headed for the waterfront, hoping to find someone who might be top dog (the German Shepherd, so to speak) of the local folklore. Because, after all, it was time to be serious and get on with the business of writing.

As it turned out, it was noon when I arrived at the harbor. At that hour of the day, there was a lot of commotion on the waterfront: seagulls flying in an undisciplined freedom, boats bobbing with each slap of the waves, fishermen unloading, cats darting and the sound of seaweeds brushing themselves against mussel-infested pilings. Despite the poetic goings-on, it would hardly have been impossible not to notice the old man, squatting by a brass brazier, grilling small palamuts—a popular fish in Turkey. He intrigued me. There were a number of things about him that suggested he wasn't your average Turkish fisherman. Of course, I had no way of knowing. But from his appearance, he could have passed for Moses.

The aromatic odor of fish, onion, lemon and dill, filtering through clouds of smoke, was enough to start my taste buds salivating. And I was hungry. The bearded man with a fringed shirt must have noticed my steady gaze and my watering mouth. Because with a gesture of the hand—an international form of communication that seldom fails—he motioned me to join him, in a jovial lively way.

Lunch was served in the open. I sat with the old man and was startled to see he wore a piece of crystal suspended by a ribbon.

"How long have you been fishing in these waters?" I asked.

"I've always been passionately fond of fishing, and probably have fished in these waters since I was ten or twelve."

"Ahhh! Then you must be quite familiar with the legend of The Lost Souls?"

"Of course, miss. Every Istanbulu knows the story. It's a very popular legend here," he answered and chuckled as though my sudden question had tickled his funny bone. He lit a cigarette and sighed deeply, as all good raconteurs do so as not to lessen the story's effect. He walked to the brazier and buried the dying embers with warm ashes.

Then the thrill of the legend lured him back to the table.

"Kucuk Hanim . . . perhaps I should tell you that there are multiple versions of the legend. As for me, I believe the report given by the sailor, who allegedly was the only person ever to see the dancing women.

"Anyway," he continued, "once the Fates—Clotho, Lachesis and Atropos—had granted a certain young sailor a perfect day to navigate his boat in the clear waters of the Marmara. Sometime before dusk, that bewitching hour when the sun dips into the water for its final hurrah, the lad dove into the sea to free an anchor that was snagged in a seaweed bed. Part way down, his eyes level with the marine hanging gardens, beyond the amphitheatre of boulders, he saw silhouettes dancing in

67

the two currents of the Bosphorus. 'Allah!' the sailor exclaimed. 'This is too magical, too weird to be true,' he told himself.

"Surfacing, at a point where the sea rises flat and blue to the horizon, he saw a flock of black birds take off from the general area where he had seen the dancing women. The birds, startled by the sudden appearance of the fisherman, flew away as silently as a spray that covers the sea after a tempest."

Meanwhile, left alone with my own thoughts, I tried to visualize the unwanted women thrown into the sea, gasping for air in tightly tied and heavily weighted sacks. What I saw wasn't pleasant; in fact it was downright barbaric and went beyond savage.

"In the ensuing years, the legend gave the birds a new identity; the souls of the unwanted harem women, who were sewn into the heavy sacks, weighted at the ankles and thrown into the strait to rendezvous with death in the dark cradle of the sea, taking with them secrets that we can only imagine. The only bright side of this legend is, those unlucky women who were separated from life so violently, were to spend eternity as beautiful water birds. To tell you the truth, it may be a folly to look for other explanations, because there are none. Hence, I will stop now, and leave you alone to think about The Lost Souls—in your own way."

"I can't thank you enough. You are a marvelous raconteur. Your devotion to legends is a rare quality to be found in the modern world that we live in. Thank you again for the story and the fish, which, by the way, was simply delicious, worthy of two stars in the Michelin Guide."

"Kucuk Hanim, the pleasure was all mine. It's not often I have lunch with such a charming lady, beautiful to boot. May God, in his kindness, unite us again," the old man said, while I gathered my notes, and descended a narrow street that skirted the walls of an ancient Greek church, a throwback from earlier times.

Luck was with me on that day in January, when I saw a publisher's ad in the Paris edition of the *Herald Tribune* for new authors. My joy turned to dismay, then to disbelief that fortune was actually smiling on me. Then I called upon the aid of God, the Merciful, to help me succeed. Not wanting to anger other lesser gods, I gave my blue eye a squeeze and sprinkled a few sesame seeds to ward off evil spirits.

Sometime in February, I wrote to the publisher in New York, to query about my book: *The Oratory of the Legends.*

Then in March the wished-for letter arrived. God, the Compassionate, must have heard my prayers. The publisher wanted my story! Praise be the Lord.

Strangely enough, the following night, just before dawn, I dreamed that Daddy was in my room. He startled me. "Poor Summer, always the consummate dreamer. Give it up, child. Because choosing to be a writer isn't going to get you anything but rejection after rejection and each rejection will crush your spirit to the point of no return. Spare yourself all that heartache and chisel a new life for yourself."

Daddy's words were like tiny demons driving hot needles into my head, but I wasn't going to let his opinion become my reality.

"No, Daddy, despite what you say, I have no intention of giving up my dreams. Now . . . what are you going to do with that?"

8

Gods cannot help those who do not seize opportunities.
—Confucius

That spring, I wrote in my diary: May was a month of many blessings. There was the day when the gardens in San Stefano turned into a sea of purple and white lilacs. And there was the day when Polson Publishing Company in New York assigned the ever popular Mr. Joel Cooper, a literary man par excellence, and one hell of a nice guy, to be my editor. My joy was boundless. This news had to be the biggest kick of a lifetime. Yippee! Now I had proof that all my prayers, tears, and my blue eye had paid off big. Because this was a wish that went beyond my wildest dreams and, as you know, reader, I had my share of them. Strangely enough, in a gush of excitement I crumbled to my knees and thanked Daddy. *But why?*

At this point, I don't wish to venture into the realm of parlor psychology—mostly because I was, and still am, the biggest dunce in the matters of human mind and animal behavior. Nonetheless, I would like to share with you my views on the emotional process that takes us beyond the frame of friendship.

It is one thing to have a lover, and another thing altogether to have a kindred spirit or, like the French love to say: *ami de l'âme*, who is completely at home within his skin, while sharing two heartbeats; his and yours. Love, like a disease, can afflict the highborn and the lowborn.

In my repository of antiques lies a small note that explains what friendship meant to me, when my flesh was young and easily bruised. It was only natural that I should write a horse show. Hmmm . . . a horse show? You may ask in wonderment. Yes, a horse show, I shall reply in a nostalgic key. However, give me a chance to explain the meaning of the horse show—before you board your broom and take off to the moon. But, in order to achieve this, I shall have to travel on my own broom, to an age of romantic innocence, and cut to the bone.

Now I am in Woodside, California, a bucolic village south of San Francisco—where mink coats and manure hold hands in the most fashionable way.

It is Saturday, and the morning of the Woodside Horse Show. I'm riding Sugar, my elegant thoroughbred mare—the handsomest of all handsome horses, a chestnut with four white stockings, huge eyes, and a kindly manner that left all the other horses in the dust. I was mostly proud of myself, because I had bought Sugar with my own pin money, a small fortune that was not to be sneezed at. Today, as it was then, horse shows are oratories to flaunt one's bravura on handsome horses.

I recall the sun dancing on the white fences and on the leafy trees. And the judge's instruction to trot our horses. I pressed my knees against Sugar's flanks as a signal for her to change her gait. My! We were such a team. We were trotting perfectly until I saw from the corner of my eye the judge's yellow umbrella swirling in a sudden gust of wind, traveling toward us. I was horrified. Sugar, having sensed my fear, panicked as well and ran away with me. As you know, horses and umbrellas rarely mix.

I leaned back and pulled in the reins, hoping to gain control of my horse. But Sugar kept on going. As we approached a tall fence, Sugar skidded to a sudden stop, which caused me to go over, but not quite, for I still had one foot in the stirrup. As Sugar tried to speed away with my foot partly in the stirrup, she narrowly missed stepping on my heart, only a few inches away. That was a close call that could have ended my life instantly.

But, you see, it wasn't my time yet.

I counted myself lucky not to be hurt physically, but mentally I was a total wreck. That freak caprice of nature cost me a blue ribbon I thought I was sure to win. Even now, after so many years when I think about that horse show, I shut my eyes and put my hands over my ears, and tell myself no, I don't ever want to relive it.

Yet, as I look back over the sad episode, I remember many things—like the way the ghosts of my dead ancestors sat on the bleachers laughing at me and the way they took turns mocking me. However, there is one bright spot that lifts my heart; then my feeling of inner joy takes over as I recall the way Uncle Hugh yelled, whistled and applauded as if I were the recipient of the much-coveted blue ribbon, the ultimate prize which slipped from my grasp that day in Woodside.

It was only natural that I returned home disillusioned. But as a whole, the experience wasn't a total bust, for it showed the other riders that I was not a person to trifle with.

All of a sudden it strikes me that the main reason for remembering that horse show was the way Uncle Hugh made me feel. To be truthful, thanks to him I felt a little taller and wiser than when I first arrived at the show, my head full of grandiose expectation to the point of feeling the blue ribbon in my hand.

Reader, if you're still wondering what is the point here, let me say that I chose a horse show because in those days horses and horse shows were the stuff of my life.

On a more personal plane, I remember the way Uncle Hugh kissed and dried my tears, confessing to me that he too had had a similar dump. Yet he mounted his horse and finished third. So what do I have to squawk about?

Years later, when I was writing my first novel, I was overtaken by a strong current of fear which can be traced to my horse show demons feasting on my brain. I was terrified of failure. It was a wonder I didn't reach for the bottle of iodine. Once again it was Uncle Hugh's sharp laugh and strong voice that saved me from throwing in the towel.

"Summer, my darling . . . is that fear I see in your eyes? That's not like you! Pull yourself together. Remember the Gold Rush . . . remember Granddad's bravado . . . he had courage and so do you. We are winners, not losers. Don't you ever forget that a Grant is never cowerer. Above all, be proud to be an American from San Francisco."

This became a credo that I spent a lifetime proving.

Meanwhile a courier arrived to Mon Plaisir with an important message. The agency needed my help to chase down a man who was a thorn in the agency's derriere. The man in question was an alleged Russian Prince, known to pass vital information to the Bolsheviks, using an underground bookstore as a front. In those days, following the Russian Revolution of 1917, murder and other strange occurrences were constantly happening outside churches where members of the Russian Imperial Family, White Russian aristocrats and opponents of bolshevism attended. The Russian crime spree was a nagging case that the agency wanted to see disappear from their files.

However, the trouble was, no one knew where to find this man. He always seemed to be one step ahead of his pursuers. He was good at what he did, always covering his bases. The agency believed the Prince hid behind fake names and frequent makeovers. Depending on whom you asked, he was last seen patronizing a certain chic brothel, Mme. Sophie's where all varieties of sex was offered in an atmosphere of old world opulence. It boasted the most gorgeous girls in the city with hourglass figures, who could converse in several tongues. They were highly paid prostitutes whose sexual prowess had no limit. In exchange, Mme. Sophie provided them a safe harbor; no one was allowed inside without the proper identification, password and a fat wallet.

An evening at Mme. Sophie's meant great sex with beautiful girls, the best champagne and heavenly hors d'oeuvres in a Byzantine richness. It is stated that more sex has been bought and sold in Mme. Sophie's salon than in any one place in the world.

However, in order to infiltrate into Mme. Sophie's pleasure domain, I first had to sell myself as an accomplished prostitute. Hence, I made an appointment to see the Queen of Night. The voice at the other end hesitated, at first. I could feel her anxiety. Finally, after much persuasion she agreed to give me a date; September 6, at 3 P.M.

I arrived at the appointed time looking drop-dead sexy. After all, sex is what I was selling. I rang the doorbell. After what seemed like an endless ring, a small door, within a large door, opened just wide enough for two eyes to give me the once-over. Obviously satisfied with my appearance, I was allowed to step inside, and ushered into an elegant salon.

The room was remarkable for its size. Two curved black lacquered stairways, at each end, led to a series of rooms that disappeared behind heavy green velvet drapes. A long gallery was painted with Chinese erotica.

After a while, Mme. Sophie appeared, holding a small white Maltese dog. She was a petite woman with a cold smile. Despite the masterly job of her maquillage, one could tell that the face had seen better times. Perhaps the most colorful side of her personality was her ability to speak five languages: Turkish, English, French, Italian and Greek. A casual observer might presume that she was quite educated, for at times she was actually quite eloquent with any one of the languages.

I managed to stay calm, while Mme. Sophie studied my reflection in the large mirror.

"I was told you sounded very anxious over the phone. What is it that you wanted? Let me hear all about it," Mme. Sophie said and leaned back on a chair. "Well . . . what can you do, miss? Putting it more bluntly; can you fuck with style? After all, this is a house of prostitution and not the Taj Mahal."

"Primarily I'm looking for work, for I spent my last lira to come here. As you can see, I'm young, pretty and can fuck with style, as you put it."

"There now, you're the sort of woman I like. Please stand up and let me examine you," Mme. Sophie said and ran her long fingers over my body. "I want to make sure what you are selling is the genuine article. I hate when girls stuff their bras with cotton, hoping to fool me. Yes, you'll do just fine. Matter of fact, I have a very important client coming tomorrow who enjoys pretty new challenges, you know what I mean. Can you start immediately?"

"Hmmm . . . I hadn't planned on it, but . . ."

"I pay in gold coins."

"That's lovely, and I sure can use the money."

"Wait. There is one more thing. The manner of life

here is strictly regulated. It's up to you to adapt to our way of life."

"I understand."

"Good. Good-bye. Please bring your prettiest clothes. I want my girls to look as stylish as any debutante who is being presented to the Queen of England. Do I make myself clear?"

"Perfectly clear. Thank you for seeing me. I appreciate the opportunity to work for you. Good-bye."

As it happened the next day was a Saturday. That morning the talk at the agency was the Prince. According to a secret communiqué the Prince was expected to arrive to Constantinople that weekend, and all was ready.

Cloaked in total secrecy, the Prince's arrival at Mme. Sophie's was late that Saturday night. Immediately, he inquired if there were any new girls who would perform oral sex. When he was told about me, he yelled with a slightly intoxicated voice, "Send her up to me. I need a pretty one who . . . especially tonight. Can she speak French?"

"French and English, too."

Thirty minutes later, I put on one of my most seductively revealing gowns. The beauty of the figure-hugging dress suited the occasion. Trailed by my own perfume, I reached room #1, always reserved for special clients, now occupied by the Prince. When I entered the interior was semi-dark, except for a small light reflecting in the bathroom mirror. A large bed, a good two feet above the floor, was covered with a silk bedspread adorned with white roses. In the uncluttered simplicity of the room, I noticed a mass of burnished gold hair lying on a large pillow. The face and the body were entirely buried in the bed.

"*Bon soir, monsieur*. I'm Mlle. Sundew, your escort," I said softly. While I waited for a reply, a scented breeze drifted in through the wooden shutters, creating the sensation of being in a garden.

"Hello," I said again—and again the Prince remained silent. His silence contributed to the atmosphere of mystery. *What is going on here?* I asked myself and stepped closer to the bed. I pulled back the bedcover. Oh, shit! what a mess. Pieces of warm flesh mixed with blood were strewn over the sheets. The entire mattress was saturated with dark red blood. I was shocked by the horror of the scene. I wasn't quite sure what had happened. But, it was evident that someone had been hiding in the room, waiting to kill the Prince.

That someone had beaten me to the draw.

A close examination revealed that the man in the bed was completely naked. And a pair of golden cufflinks with double-headed eagles was on the floor . . .

For months I forgot about the Prince and the cufflinks. The case was marked closed, yet still open for me. None of this was taken lightly. Then six months later, someone pushed a note under Pomme d'Or's door. It was written on fine stationery, the kind used by the gentry. It simply said:

I had to shoot him. Consider yourself lucky. You can't expect to be lucky every time, you know. The son of a bitch is dead. This puts an end to the hunt. I shall remain anonymous. But I want you to know that I'm a White Russian, whose father was hung by his balls until dead, by a Bolshevik Commissar. The killing of the Prince, who turned against his own people, was a remorseless pleasure. Long Live Mother Russia!

The following day I took refuge in my writing. Winter in Constantinople can be as fickle as a mistress. On that particular day, despite the forecast for clear weather, dark clouds were painting the sky with the entire spectrum of the gray that nobody could duplicate. Dressed in a full-length Russian lynx coat (de rigueur then) I headed for the city in pursuit of new material for my book in progress. Before long, I was tramping snow-covered sidewalks nudging my way past shoppers as colorful as the furs they were wearing. The air crackled with the threat of a storm ready to spring at any moment. Sure enough, before I could identify snow, a deluge of hailstones bombarded the street with a vengeance. And an icy wind blowing from the north forced me to seek shelter in an eclectic bookstore where in the center of the room stood a stove radiating heat evenly. All available space was festooned with pictures of Loti, Proust, Daudet and Sarah Bernhardt—all past habitués of the bookstore.

With that certain élan of a writer's bravura, I approached a ziggurat of small books tottering on a round table with impressive claw feet. These included some great literature printed in a multitude of languages. Among them a leather bound book, engraved with gold letters, which seemed to have a narcissistic world of its own, jumped out from the others to capture my attention. *Sultans and Sultanas*: a simple enough title that gave basis for expecting the unexpected.

I was in my element.

I sat on a chair opposite a life-size effigy of Loti, perhaps the best-loved French writer in Turkey, dressed in one of his Turkish costumes. The apparatus could be set in motion by simply pressing a small handle. Loti was almost a religion in Constantinople. I gave my imagination free rein and started to peruse *Sultans and Sultanas*. With each turn of the page, the past and the present merged together in a most curious way, taking me on a wild pursuit as breathtaking as a ride on a Ferris wheel with a broken axle.

One minute I was having tea with Roxelana, Sultan Suleiman's red-headed Russian wife, at the Grand Seraglio, and the next minute I was lunching with Aimee Dubucq de Rivery, Queen Mother of Sultan Mahmut and the cousin of Josephine Bonaparte; all within a book, within a space and within a store. Truly, exciting. Even in my craziest dreams, I could have imagined such a journey back in history.

Outside, the wind had subsided. A hard-to-describe hush lay over the city. I paid the clerk and left the bookstore, my eyes blinded by falling snow. To tell the truth, I was glad to be out of that store where the smell of garlic fought with the scent of the expensive French perfume, Heure Bleu, now the rave of the chic glitterati. As for me, I preferred an anonymous Turkish scent, as mysterious as a woman behind a veil, which was dispensed out of a large bottle at Monsieur Angeliki's whatnot shop located in San Stefano's main street. Monsieur Angeliki's was not a fancy place like the Jean Patou boutique in Paris. Each time you entered, you saw the shop differently, depending what mood you were in. I can't imagine that part of the country without the funky stores that propel one into a fantasy world.

In front of Galata Saray in Pera, almost kitty-cornered from the British Embassy (the educational institution for the aristocratic Turkish boys, who regard Osmanlik as their divine heritage), I hailed a taxi. It was a whimsical vehicle painted black, yellow and orange, with a colorful driver to match its éclat.

"Hanim, do you have any cigarettes?" the driver asked eagerly.

"I'm sorry, no. I don't smoke. But I have gum."

"Oh, never mind me. Sometimes I get so bored, I puff on cigarettes to chase away ennui. The life of a taxi driver isn't what it is cracked up to be."

"Well, nothing in life is as it appears from the outside."

"I don't know about you, but most of my days are filled with humdrum talk and argumentative people, who tell you how to drive."

"That's life."

"I suppose you're right, hanim."

Despite the taxi's astounding paint job and the age of the driver, it juggernauted over the Galata Bridge, honking and dodging pedestrians who were scurrying to secure seats on the evening ferries, zigzagging both sides of the Bosphorus—like the cranes that carry swallows in the deep hollows of their bodies (as legend has it).

I arrived at the Sirkeci Station just in time to catch the 6:15 operating at the peak of the commuter hour. The train's cars, from first class to third class, were filled with the usual eclectic crowd: commuters dressed in suits with shiny seats; uniformed students from English, French, Italian, German and Turkish high schools, laden with books; and a few now-and-then travelers who were returning to their villages bogged down with bundles and boxes.

In those bygone days, one's eyes feasted well in the first-class compartments with their comfortable leather seats. These drawing rooms on wheels, as they were called then, were always clamorous with baritone and high-pitched voices, cigarette smoke, and the smell of humanity. One of the things that never failed to fascinate me was the parade of the Russian aristocracy who walked like ciphers with eyes wearing blinkers, dreaming of the memory of their former lives in Russia, lives that now existed only in fairy tales.

In the panoply of exotic nationals, the Italians never disappointed me. The theatrics of their gestures were equivalent to hundreds of spoken words. And the Italian women were reputed to be the best-dressed women in Constantinople.

Then came the French. They were an amusing flock, but not at the expense of others. All in all, they comprised a vivid tableau of a particular segment of society in the early twentieth century.

Despite the varied and rich experience, and the battle of many tongues, I must have been in communication with my Muse. Because by the time the train huffed and puffed into San Stefano, I had an entire chapter filed in my head, dedicated to my fellow travelers who had provided me with another facet of daily life more fascinating than anything I might have imagined.

Outside, the darkness was forbiddingly cold. As if to make up for the weather's foulness, snow-dusted phaetons, waiting for fares in front of the station, were burning their lanterns brighter than usual, perhaps trying to give the arriving passengers a false sense of warmth. The shimmering lanterns, reminiscent of the one in the Seven Dwarves' cottage, were wonderful antidotes for a night cold enough to freeze a crow in mid-flight, or chase a pack of wolves back into their dens.

The freezing temperature of that night wasn't for the faint of heart, yet how could one not love the dancing snowflakes in the pines, surrounding Mon Plaisir? *Au contraire*, the house was toasty warm and reeked of garlic-stuffed roast lamb coated with majoram. When Uncle Hugh heard that I was in the vestibule, he rushed out of the library and threw his arms around my shivering body.

"Summer, darling I missed you! Without you I'm as lonely as a bee without its queen," he said as he helped me out of my boots.

"Gee whiz, I was only away for a few hours. It's not as though I was gone for years! On the other hand, it's nice to know that you've missed me. In truth, I've missed you, too."

"I feel so incomplete without you," he continued, inhaling deeply the new perfume behind my ears. He was about to skip over reality and into ecstasy—when Boris stuck his head into the room and said, "Good evening, Mademoiselle Grant. I must say! You look very smart in your lynx coat, but a bit flushed. I hope you are not coming down with the grippe that's been going around?"

"I don't think so. Thanks for asking, though. Really, I'm fit as a fiddle . . . but famished."

"Fit as a fiddle? *Mon Dieu!* What does that mean? To tell you the truth, I simply cannot keep up with all your American slang," Boris said with respect and wonderment.

"There is nothing to worry about. I'm the healthiest woman in San Stefano. Fit as a fiddle means—well and healthy. And this is the best winter ever."

"America and Russia are so different, yet very similar. But I believe you Americans, despite your polished façades, are . . . *comment on dit . . . quelque chose peu drole. Oui, c'est necessaire* that I learn your lingo in order to understand you better. Don't you agree?"

"Absolutely, Boris."

"Necessity knows no law," Uncle Hugh said and laid another adage on Boris.

"Monsieur . . . I'm quite familiar with that old saying, also popular in Russia."

"Well, Boris, what's for dinner?" Uncle Hugh asked

curiously, suddenly overtaken by hunger pains.

Boris flashed a perfect smile and answered, "All good, Monsieur. Tonight I feel very proud of myself. In fact, happy enough to sing an ode to my lamb."

"Now, my man, that's a treat."

"And for you, Madamoiselle Grant, I have a big surprise."

"What is it? Don't keep me in suspense, please."

"It's apple pie à la American with home-made vanilla ice cream."

"Wow! Ice cream in the depth of winter? I'm touched. Darn! There goes my waistline . . . but . . . what the heck. You only live once. Just for tonight let us pretend there are no calories in ice cream."

"I agree."

"Boris, I consider myself lucky to be your friend. You are a national treasure. Because you're unlike anyone that I've ever met."

"Thank you Monsieur for saying so."

"My pleasure, indeed."

Despite the passage of many moons and voices forever silenced, Boris is very much alive in my heart. Boris, who believed eternity was each passing minute, passed away at the age of 65, after battling a malignant brain tumor.

9

For half so boldly can the no man Swere and lyen
as a woman can.
—Chaucer's Prologue

I cannot imagine what prompted me to suddenly remember a knee-jerk insanity—an image I cannot forget—when I appeared on the scene wearing nothing but a garland of creamy gardenias on my head.

It all started sometime after dark.

Once, many years ago, I was burning the midnight oil, reading the intriguing memoirs of Abdi, the Turkish historian and the favorite of Sultan Mahomet in 1595, when a sudden release gave me a way to act out a feeling that filled me to bursting.

"Summer, darling. I'm beginning to think I've lost you to the Ottoman Sultans," Uncle Hugh's voice echoed from the adjoining room like a sharp razor in the hands of a newbie. "Summer, please . . . tell me that you still love me."

"What are you talking about? Of course I love you, you silly bear."

"Don't let me disturb you, but I miss you."

"Please be quiet and let me work," I pleaded.

"Okay. But for how long?"

"Gosh! I don't know. But not before I put my finger on why I don't like Sultan Mahomet. Once I find out, I won't strain my eyeballs, nor strive so hard for the truth."

"If you're not hammering out the details now, you soon will be. So what's the big urgency?"

"If I knew, there would be no need to ask the question myself."

"I have no evidence to back this up, but I've got a gut feeling that you are more interested in your Sultans than in me. Can that be?"

"Hogwash. You know darn well that's not true."

"Can I have a kiss?"

"Yes, yes, all right," I replied and placed my lips on his. My lust, forgotten amidst the silly conversation, flamed anew at the touch of his hands caressing my body.

"Summer, your kiss was electric. Now go while you've still got the chance—before this moment turns into a grand passion."

"Right," I said and returned to my desk.

"Summer... what sort of man do you like? Am I too old for you?"

"You, old? Never, my darling. Now if you keep quiet for an hour, and let me work in peace, I'll make your wait worthwhile."

"Is that a promise?"

"Of course, unless you break your end of the bargain."

"Oh, dear! That sounds so mysterious and naughty."

"Well... I suppose it is. But the ticklish part is yet to come."

"Okay. So let the count begin."

"Hmmmm... you are shameless and terrible. Have I ever told you that?"

"Only a hundred million times. Blessed is the man who can recognize love in all its disguises."

"Really?"

Of course I was fibbing. Because, you see, I already

knew why I disliked Sultan Mahomet who, by the law of fratricide, had ordered the strangulation of his nineteen brothers, the eldest only eleven, with that special Ottoman custom—The Silken Bowstring—because no royal blood must ever be spilled. I felt ashamed that I had lied. So why had I lied? Go and burn a candle to the God I've sinned against. Come on, hold on to your candle and let me explain. Bookworms with curious minds like me are usually happy to spend an entire night with their books, preferring them to human company. Ironically, the other reason is to make sex sexier for that special occasion when anticipation is half the fun.

I glanced at my watch. It was 2 A.M. I was really glad time had passed so quickly. "I'm off," I said, rising. "I have a promise to keep."

I ran into the bathroom to begin the beauty ritual of the harem women, who were well-versed in the art of pleasing their masters. So I took upon myself the pleasant task of making myself as alluring as any odalisque being prepared to bed with a sultan.

I bathed and scrubbed my entire body with a scented paste of rice flour, rose water and almond oil until my skin glowed with a pinkish sheen. I creamed and perfumed every inch of my body, rimmed my eyes with kohl and applied a shocking pink lipstick, a new Parisian color several shades brighter than my usual shade of delicate coral. I became one of those French cocodettes of the demimonde who sell sex for francs. A mysterious delight took possession of me as I saw my reflection in the mirror. I felt not only gorgeous, but ravishing enough for any sultan to place a handkerchief on my shoulder, an indication that I was the object of his passion—at least for that night. This unfamiliar image of myself took me by surprise, since I had never been known for my vanity. I smiled with narcissistic glee and assured the me inside me that she was indeed a beautiful package: full lips, dreamy eyes, big-nippled breasts as fresh as sparkling morning dew on the leaves, a compact derrière with its own brand of wiggle. In a word: enchanting.

I closed my eyes, satisfied as a bee plunging into the flowers. Everything around me became a fantasy as I wondered about a grand entrance that was suitable for a femme fatale as devastating as me. That said, hold on to your yashmaks (veils) because you are in for a big surprise and you are going to need your yashmaks to cover your eyes in pretend modesty.

"Oh God! You are a sight for sore eyes, if you don't mind my saying so," Uncle Hugh exclaimed as I burst into the room wearing my own skin, roses around my neck and gardenias in my hair. He looked at me in total shock, but tried to laugh it off.

As for me, I was having such a good time being the new me! In my mind I saw myself as a beautiful study in nudity. However, from the look of things, I wasn't sure whether Uncle Hugh was sharing my enthusiasm. Regardless of what he thought, my own boldness became one of my most treasured possessions to remember on dark days.

"Hello . . . is anyone here?" I asked Uncle Hugh, who seemed to be miles away.

After a while he smiled and started to whistle a strange tune. "Honestly, I'd never imagined that you had it in you to be so wild. I'm speechless!"

Suddenly, I felt a blush beginning to suffuse my cheeks. I had gambled my clothes on the bold scheme, hoping to please Uncle Hugh, whose gratification had been postponed. But now I wondered if this was such a good idea.

"Perhaps I was a bit too wild and vulgar. But, on the other hand, there was no harm done and I won't be cast into hell. I thought it might please you to see me so abandoned."

"Apparently, you succeeded."

"I had hoped to get a bigger rise out of you."

"Oh, really?"

"Yes, really."

"Okay, okay . . . you look terrific—in an abstract way."

"Perhaps I should go back and come in again?"

"There's no need for that. To be honest, you look as tempting as an exotic wahine. Now *that* should please you! In fact, for a moment I thought I was back in Bora Bora, admiring a lovely native with a hibiscus behind her ear."

"Bora Bora? For God's sake, when were you in Polynesia?"

"Long time ago. Now the memory of Bora Bora is just a pebble that stopped skipping over the water when you came to Constantinople. I'd much rather be with you than all the wahines in the South Pacific."

"Do you really mean it?"

"Of course, I do, you silly twit. Here . . . come and sit by me and I'll prove to you how much I love you," Uncle Hugh said, patting the pillows on the sofa.

"Okey-doke. But first let me cover myself with this robe—just in case Gauguin walks in and decides to immortalize me in oils," I replied and reached for the silk robe on the chair.

As I stood up, I caught a glimpse of myself in the large mirror. Even under the soft electric light, I looked as ridiculous as a bird stripped of its plumage, or perhaps more like a hairless dog with a pinkish skin. Let me tell you, reader, it's not easy to see yourself in that fashion. If

I were a copper-skinned wahine wearing an orchid lei, this picture of myself would have been as easy on the eye as the beautiful Aphrodite who arose from the sea fully grown with a divine body. But, the naked truth was: I could never be anything but an Anglo-American woman with lily-white skin and blonde pubic hair.

Triggered into action, Uncle Hugh began caressing and kissing every dimple of my body. I trembled all over. I looked around me. We were alone somewhere in Polynesia, in a blue-green lagoon, floating between gentle waves, our bodies glued together by the heat of our passion. It was miraculous.

When we emerged from the imaginary lagoon, I remembered nothing; it was as if I had been given chloroform. Despite my hallucinatory state, I swear my hair was wet, my skin covered with scented droplets of water and my nose tickled with the perfume of tiara-miri and its aromatic leaves. For a split second I wondered where I was. Then I heard Uncle Hugh's voice and that lassoed me from fantasy to reality.

"Happy?"

"Wildly happy; and you?"

"Never happier in my life," Uncle Hugh said dreamily, his eyes fixed on the ceiling in a celestial bliss, luxuriating in passion's afterglow. "It was quite an adventure."

"Was it as good for you as it was for me?" I asked.

"It was a marvelous experience. Listen, this will make you laugh, but before we go on another journey, I want to make sure I bring along a fig leaf and rub my skin with walnut oil."

"Lord, have mercy on me!"

The Polynesian interlude disappeared eventually, as all fantasies do, with the arrival of a new day. Somewhere in the grass a frog was serenading the rising sun. For me, the sound of a croaking frog always brings back memories—like the time when I fell into a pond at the Red Poppy.

Once, a billion years ago, I almost captured a frog that was napping quietly on a slippery rock. I don't know why I wanted that frog, but I just did. So I zeroed in on it. Just when I thought I had the frog, it leaped into the water, taking me with it. I fell like a lead balloon between clusters of water lilies and into the murky depths of the silt. The smell of the stagnant water stuck to me like some cheap perfume. And to make matters worse, LeRoy, a boy who made my heart beat faster than a pinwheel in a hurricane, appeared on the scene right after the muddy imbroglio, groomed immaculately as if he had just stepped out from the pages of a men's fashion magazine. It was a hair-raising moment with a quickened heartbeat.

10

Mysteries are not necessarily miracles.
                                        —Goethe

Now something else rushes back to me—a curiosa of
sorts—of a style and charm found almost exclusively in
books of yore.

Each year autumn bestows on San Stefano a robe of
many colors; its threads impregnated with the scents of
ripe persimmon, quince and ruby pomegranate.

To be honest, up to that point, I hadn't given much
thought to autumn, nor to the splendor of its broad-scope
flamboyance, despite being a visual person. I cannot tell
you why I picked that particular day to look for another
legend—when my coffers were already bulging with all
sorts of fascinating stories, enough to enchant generations yet to come.

On that typical autumnal afternoon, I was taken
entirely into San Stefano's religious past, and I knew I
must go now and look for Aya Fotini's Chapel. The road
leading to the chapel was paved with slippery cobbles.
And flowers were everywhere. They gave life to the tall
grapevines, growing helter-skelter against weathered
wooden houses with minaret-like pinnacles.

I questioned the degree of my conviction as I stood by
the doorway of a house covered with scaly paint, wondering whether to go in or not. I asked myself, what's the
worst that can happen? I might see a phantom or a

hunchback—like the Hunchback of Notre Dame—who emerges from the dark shadows and whisks me away to a secret chamber.

Beyond the pair of wooden doors hung a plaque proclaiming this to be Aya Fotini's Chapel. Shudders, like powerful waves, crushed over me as I made my way toward a narrow hall, emptying into an equally narrow room. The play of light, filtering through the iron barred window, reminded me of those painted Russian eggs nesting inside each other that grow more beautiful as they get smaller. Gratefully, I was alone with a devout old lady in total black, who crossed herself again and again as if she were listening to the reading of the Gospels.

Meanwhile I walked with a big, black cockroach that lumbered slowly down the stone steps, oblivious to its surroundings, except for its shadow trudging behind.

The interior of the chapel was eerily quiet and it seemed like the afternoon might be predictably uneventful. Beyond the mass of burning candles, hundred of *tamatas*—silver offerings—tucked all around a large Byzantine style icon, shimmered in the candles' glow. I stood by the icon, painted in the likeness of Aya Fotini, and wondered about what sort of wishes these tamatas represented. And if Aya Fotini would grant the pilgrims' wishes in exchange for some vow? In Shakespeare's words: The miserable have no other medicine but hope.

With the boldness one has in dreams, I sank to my knees, crossed myself and looked the Saint square in the eyes. It seemed as though the Saint herself had her eyes focused on me, too. Perhaps she was wondering what I was canvassing for. Suddenly, I realized that the Saint was following me with her eyes as I reached for the bucket of Holy Water drawn from a well in the room. At that moment she seemed as if she were an actual physical incarnation of a divine presence. I took several sips.

The water seemed pure and was sparkling clear. There wasn't any hint of unpleasant taste or odor. With each sip, I felt goose bumps on the back of my neck and all the way down to my feet. I pondered for a few minutes before bargaining with the Saint.

"Please, dear Saint...I need to find happiness through the forgiveness of my sins. In exchange for your kindness, I will support the orphanage of the handicapped children, on your behalf. I hope this promise will please you." I gazed into her eyes. Strangely enough in her stare I found her answer. I was very relieved that she had heard me.

Soon after my talk with the Saint, I heard a popping sound echoing from the icon. Almost at that moment I thought of the Greek Orthodox priest, who told me, "If an icon makes a noise, it's because the Saint is giving you a sign that your request will be granted."

It's anyone's guess whether Aya Fotini heard me or not. I cannot say for sure, yet I want to believe that a divine being communicated with me, on that day in the chapel.

Now, as I look back, another puzzling question stands up to be counted. Did I really hear that sound? Despite my belief in the power of prayer, a lot of question marks appear before my eyes. Do I believe in the legend of Aya Fotini? And the miraculous properties of the water? My answer to these questions is yes. Why should this be so? Because certain changes have occurred in my life, all for the better, since my visit to Aya Fotini.

Also, in my lifetime, I have witnessed amazing healings credited to Aya Fotini. Perhaps this is why I continue to believe in her and in the power of her miracles. So I came to the conclusion that I must definitely join the choir of angels, who are constantly singing the praise of God and His Saints.

Therefore, before you erect your spines by inflating yourself with doubt, take a few minutes to listen to the voice of wisdom: If you have faith as a grain of mustard seed, ye shall say unto this mountain, remove hence to yonder places; and it shall remove.

—Matthew 17:20

I hope to God I'm right.

11

To me the meanest flower that blows can give
thoughts that do often lie too deep for tears.
                                    —Wordsworth

A long chain of events followed my visit to Aya Fotini's
subterranean chapel with its ever-burning lampadas and
its medley of silver offerings.

As I began to think about a new chapter for *The Oratory of the Legends*, flowers came to mind, followed by
Yesil Park—halfway up the Bosphorus, between the
Golden Horn and the Black Sea.

Yesil Park, as it was called in those days, was a primo
destination of botanists searching for a certain plant, or
for legend buffs trying to unravel the centuries-old mystery of the Water Lily's legend, allegedly born in the park.

At any time of the year, Constantinople is a warehouse of legends. But in the spring it is Yesil Park that
hurls itself at nature and becomes a never-ending book of
fairly tales. And it doesn't take much to call forth visions
of fairies, talking dragonflies and giant spiders capable of
building entire villages of web.

Hence on that particularly lovely spring day festooned with puffy cloudlets, when visions of flowers
danced in my head, Yesil Park seemed the logical place to
start.

So entranced was I by the sight of the park that its
memory lingered vividly up to the time when I wrote in

95

my diary: As the sun rose up the sky, the ferry pulled into the harbor, replete with outdoor cafés and winding paths planted with ancient pines and a few Johnny-come-latelies with interesting names, yet lacking the rich patina of time. Wild pear trees lined the road to the park. Inside the park I saw beautiful red and white tulips corseting small bodies of water. Among the rocks yellow daffodils and irises extended themselves like ostrich feather fans.

The unreal quality of this visual feast was enough to push the limits of my talent.

The high point of the day was the man standing among fragrant lilac bushes, looking as if he were a part of the backdrop. The effect was quite amazing.

"Merhaba Bayan," the man said, and came to greet me. "What brings you to the park on such a warm day? By the way, are you the American lady who called me from the harbor, wishing to see the water lilies? I'm Ali Hasan, the head gardener," he continued, his voice in perfect harmony the way a man of flowers should sound.

"Ali Bey, you are absolutely right. I'm that American lady."

"Ahhh . . . so you are. I'm honored, indeed, that you came to our park. The park has changed quite a bit in the fifteen years I've known it. But its spirit has remained high, because the lilies growing here are the best in the world, let alone the legend. Pray tell me why you singled out the lily? After all, our park is famous for its birds, also."

"Coming here was a private dream come true. You see, I'm doing research on a book on legends."

"Well . . . that makes sense," he answered, beaming like a proud father who sees his firstborn through a hospital's nursery window for the first time. "Please follow me, Let's sit here," he said, pointing to a large boulder. "This is the exact spot that brought the water lilies into prominence." The boulder was carved with figures dating back to the time when Constantinople was the largest city in Medieval Europe.

"Ali Bey, you have such good command of the English language. It's a pleasure to converse with you. The whimsical quality of your pronunciation is such a delight to the ears."

"Thank you. It's very flattering to one's ego to hear you say that. You see, I lived in England for two years. I guess some of that English accent rubbed off on me."

"England? What were you doing in England?"

"After graduating from San Benoit in Galata, I was fortunate enough to be a protégé of the great botanist Oliver Howard, who recognized my passion before anyone else did, and through him I was invited to England as an apprentice at the Botanical Gardens in Bath."

"So . . . you speak French, too?"

"*Oui. Cela va sans dire.*"

"In truth, Mr. Howard was an individual of immense talent, wit and charm, as well as the possessor of a very large fortune. Upon his death, he bequeathed the bulk of his estate to the Botanical Society, for the preservation of water lilies. He was effortlessly generous to any preoccupation that he loved and that interested him."

"That was very noble of him."

"Yes, one can say that."

"However, there is an interesting coda to Mr. Howard's life: although he was inspired to give away his entire riches to the lilies, he totally ignored the other flowers. That haunted my life for so many years. To make a long story short, I got the job here because of his passion for the water lilies."

I noticed for the first time that the midday sun had fallen over the pond like a golden veil. Immediately, two frogs jumped into the water. The impact created deep fissures between showy pink and white water lilies, looking like floating icebergs on the water.

"I hate to break the spell, but would you like a cup of coffee?" Ali Bey asked as he stood up to help a young boy carrying a round brass tray laden with two small cups of Turkish coffee, two glasses of water and a dish of pistachio lokum.

"Sure, I'd love a cup," I said softly, while trying to concentrate all my attention on the dragonflies feeding on mosquitoes congregating on the pond. It goes without saying that I was touched by Ali's generosity, but it didn't surprise me. After all, Turks are the most hospitable people in the world. They offer you tea, coffee and gazoz at the drop of a hat.

Ali Bey wiped the beads of sweat from his forehead and chased away a tiny butterfly that was tickling his ears. Unhurriedly, almost lovingly, he sipped his coffee, lit a cigarette and inhaled deeply.

"Here in our ponds we grow every known variety of water lily," he said. "An interesting footnote," he added as he munched on a lokum. "Water Lily bears a strange resemblance to a barometer. In many countries water lilies are used in forecasting changes in the weather. I cannot explain how they do it, but I know that they do. In my notes for a yet-to-be published book on flowers, I recount 'The Legend of the Water Lily' with all the passion of a man in love with his flowers—to the point of arrogance."

"You, Ali Bey, are a consummate romantic—when it comes to flowers," I said and flipped into the air a leaf lying on my lap.

"Now on with the story. According to an old folktale which made light of darkness during its heyday—once upon a time, then, there was a little princess named Gulbahar, who was as frail as a newborn sparrow with downy feathers. Gulbahar hated the cold, the wind and the ice of the winter. Hence, one day in utter desperation, she turned to her friend, Water Lily—it was the first time she ever talked to a flower—to see if it could send her a message of some sort, that would warn her about the severity and the length of winters. Of course, Water Lily obliged, rustling its large petals like wings and saying, 'A delicate princess like you doesn't belong in a cold place like this.'

"So, now, when a water lily blooms in early summer, it is simply saying that summer will be long, dry and a scorcher. On the other hand, when the water lily sheds its blossoms early in the fall, it is warning not only the little princess, but all gardeners that winter will be cold and long." At this point, Ali Bey stopped and smiled as he saw a flock of migratory birds land on the pool on their way to Africa. A noticeable sense of relief swept over him when they suddenly flew into the immovable axis of the sky, leaving the pond to the dragonflies feeding on mosquitoes.

"You see, Water Lily was the princess's friend to the very end. Some say—like Scheherazade in *Thousand and One Nights*—Water Lily earned her rank of Chosen. To this day, fans still come to leave flowers at the pond's edge, in memory of Water Lily who was staggeringly beautiful. This is according to the historians.

"As for me, my own romance with the water lily started on one hot summer day, when I fell into a pond and came face to face with a bunch of floating water lilies. There and then I was smitten with their beauty."

I watched with utter fascination as the sun dipped

into the water without an iota of braggadocio. Water lily and sunset may be little things, but at that hour of the day, they're part of a legend.

"By the way, did I mention that I was writing a book on Turkish legends—stories that enchanted many generations of Turks?" I asked.

"What a wonderful idea. But no book of legends is complete unless Water Lily is part of it."

"Of course. That is exactly what I intend to do."

"I wish you lots of success. May all your characters sprout wings and carry your book up the ladder of fame. Now, however, I must leave you to be still and quiet with yourself. *Allahaismarladik.*"

"*Gule gule*, Ali Bey. Thank you for your time. I saw and heard more than I ever imagined," I replied and waved as he walked across a small meadow.

Needless to say, I returned to the park soon after *The Oratory of the Legends* was published. Not surprisingly Ali Bey greeted me with open arms, announcing happily that coffee was ready. After a short walk with lizards and birds, we found a pergola ensconced in its own fragrant rose bed. Its purity was a long leap from Constantinople, where nearly everything moves to the beat of a faster drummer.

If by chance you happen to be in Rumeli Hisar, make a point of visiting Yesil Park. Who knows? Maybe you will imbibe its colorful past and feel the texture of the paint for a novel you are about to write.

12

So many worlds, so much to do
So little done, such things to do.
              —Lord Tennyson

As time cuts, chips and hews the years, time has become my worst enemy. It mocks me. It laughs at my reflection in the mirror, caked with powder and lipstick bleeding into the fine lines of my lip contour area. Since dementia is the disease of old age, I must hurry and jot down all that's still fresh in my memory, before darkness comes crashing down on me.

I remember once being told that God created the acacia with Constantinople in mind. Since then the city fought hard to make the acacia the great success that it became.

Trying now to recreate in my memory a certain day in July, the first thing that comes to mind is the warmth of the creamy acacia clusters growing outside my windows. I didn't start out loving acacias naturally; it was a taste I acquired after my arrival in Constantinople.

The Day of the Acacia occurs at about the same time as the American Fourth of July. On that day as I headed toward Café Ops (now coming back into the social scene as the place to be seen), I tried to guess the identity of the man sitting on a chair, his face hidden behind a newspaper. Perhaps what attracted me most was the quality of his quiet laughter which ranged from whimsical to classical. His style, though different, amused me. And that may explain why I took a table kitty-cornered from his, yet far enough to observe him without being too obvious. Besides the man, the café abounded with interesting people, dressed in *dernier cri* clothes. Because of my passion for observing humanity in all its forms, I took no notice that the mysterious man had departed as silently as the b in debt.

On any given day, Café Ops reverberates with the conversation of a new breed of literary intellectuals, who gather there for the battle of opinions. With a few exceptions, most of the White Russian officers made daily stops at the café to enjoy cups of tea without charge. Usually, they congregated behind a large screen hung with surrealistic paintings by lesser known artists.

As I sat there absorbed in my thoughts, suddenly I realized the Russians were discussing Gustave Flaubert and his influence on other writers—Thomas Mann, Emile Zola, Alphonse Daudet—and other literary men of passion. In my small circle of friends that was very important.

Meanwhile, at the far end of Café Ops a drama of another color was playing—between a man with an ugly carbuncle over his left eye and a woman with cutaway shoes and heels painted pink. For a while I let my eyes dance on their faces. Soon they became a smoky blur, and my imagination was unable to rise to the challenge.

Despite the veneer of fashion, there was something very intriguing about the couple. I wondered about their conversation. Why were they discussing Leon Trotsky with such zeal? Were they a part of a bigger conspiracy that was planning to kill Trotsky in Mexico City, where he had settled in 1937 after being accused of treason by Stalin? Perhaps it was this kind of curiosity that had inspired Agatha Christie to invent the famous detective Hercule Poirot.

I cringe when I realize that my own vivid imagination had turned the couple into would-be criminals; for all I knew they were two people interested in world affairs.

Now on the scene longer than I imagined, I left the café to the Russians and the mysterious couple and made my way to Pomme d'Or. A large shipment of books was due to arrive that afternoon at three, a gift from Mme. de Guyenne, who wrote novels under the name of Eugenie de Currier. Thanks to her generosity, I could indulge my craving for antique books I never dreamed of getting my hands on in Constantinople.

Mme. de Guyenne's books were selling fast. The sale went on and on until there was not a single volume left.

Later that afternoon at the Pomme d'Or, while I was still caught in the spell of the books, I heard a man's voice addressing me from across the room.

"Pardon, mademoiselle . . . is the phoenix a symbol of immortality, or a bird that marks the spot where a treasure might be buried?" the voice asked. I responded without bothering to look up to see to whom I was talking. Yet the name that kept coming up was Salih.

"Monsieur, it all depends whether you believe the Egyptian myth, or the Chinese myth, or the Imperial Ottoman sign," I replied in French, the language of choice of the Turkish elite. I often got into linguistic jams and had to be rescued by someone, but this was long after the days when I could barely hold my own in French. By now I spoke French well enough to converse with the best of them.

"Monsieur, regardless of your belief, the phoenix in your hand is an exquisite jade bird belonging to the Tang Dynasty."

"Mademoiselle, I'm more up to believe the Imperial Ottoman sign. For it is the symbol of death and resurrection of the Imperial Sons of Osman," the man explained, still without revealing his face.

In the meantime, I returned to my desk, but kept an eye on the man, who then said, "Mademoiselle, this phoenix is much too lovely for me to let pass. I'll take it!" And at that moment he exposed his face—until now hidden by the brim of his hat.

"Good God! I thought it might be you, Salih but I wasn't sure! It's nice to see you. What brings you back to Constantinople?"

"Well . . . all is not right in my life. Little did I know that Paris wasn't the answer to my prayers. I was lonely, so I had to return to you, for you're the energy that takes me beyond myself. I can no longer play the piano; you're driving me mad with love."

"Salih . . . please control yourself. Would you like a cup of tea?"

"No, thanks, I don't need tea, I need my arms around you. I must talk to you in private. Can we meet later at the Marquis? The Marquis is safe."

"Of course. Are you still concerned about your safety? You seem to be at such a low ebb."

"As I've told you, the Armenians are determined to kill me to avenge the horors inflicted on them by my father. Death, at an early age, is a confirmed part of my destiny. And on some future day, they will succeed. Events will unfold on their own, whether we like them or not."

"Salih, perhaps you're too consumed with the Armenians. And maybe you're putting the whole thing out of proportion," I said, never, never imagining such a horrendous fate for a man who was as gentle as a spring rain on roses.

(However, many years later, I was told by one of Salih's friends that there had been several attempts to kill him. Each time the alleged assassin was an Armenian, but never apprehended.)

"Strangely enough, sometimes in my mind's eye I see myself lying in a dark pit. I feel my body turning into dust and a new life growing above me. I truly believe the Gypsy was right when she told me I will never grow old to see my hair turn white. Silly, isn't it?"

"Stop it! You'll probably live long enough to see a man walking on the moon. I'll see that you do. By the way, what time shall we meet at the Marquis?" I asked.

"How about five?"

"Five is a good number. I will be there."

"Good-bye, Summer. You are everything that makes my life a reality," Salih said and left the Pomme d'Or as nonchalantly as an ordinary man going about his business.

I was enchanted by the thought of meeting Salih at the Patisserie Marquis. There is no better source in Constantinople for the world's best cakes, chocolates and sugar-coated walnuts. As for romance—to be continued later.

Throughout the years, Marquis has maintained its old world atmosphere and managed to hang on to "Le Printemps," a lovely panel inspired by the paintings of Alphone Mucha, the famous Czech artist of the Art Nouveau era. Le Printemps is capable of taking you wherever you wish to go—from the South Pole to the Caribbean—while you remain seated in your chair, imagining yourself in some exotic place, and thinking that perhaps you're hearing the breathing of a bee while being fed beebread.

On that warm sunny day in July, however, as Salih and I settled in a dark booth on comfortable cane chairs, we ordered a pot of tea and an assortment of cookies that were recent offerings at the patisserie. The conversation at the table centered around the Music Conservatoire in Paris, a subject about which I knew next to nothing, and also the Armenians, another current topic.

A waiter, who complemented the interior by Raoul Pasquale, his allure made more conspicuous by the cut of his pants, was at our table within minutes, taking great delight in offering Salih all sorts of little iced petit-fours, at the same time ignoring me to the point of annoyance. However, I kept on nibbling on delicate madeleines, too delicious to resist.

When we were alone, finally, Salih leaned toward me and whispered into my ear a few endearing words that took me off guard and made me lose my composure. Honestly, I didn't mean to do it, but I laughed, spilling tea all over my new white skirt.

You see, reader, nothing prepares you for a man like Salih.

Despite the passing of many years, I still laugh remembering Salih's words, spoken from the heart.

"Did I miss something funny?"

"I'm sorry. Your whispered words tickled my heart, that's all."

"How can you be so amused at a time like this?"

"Like what?"

"Like I'm crazy for you."

"Shush! You don't even know who I am. When you look at me, you only see what you want to see. I'm a woman who wears many hats, and is as complex as the works of a clock."

"I don't have to know anything about you. Your past is your own. It has nothing to do with here and now. Don't you understand that?"

"Sure, but . . ."

"No buts, please."

"That's really very big of you."

"From the first moment I met you, I haven't had a moment's peace. Your face haunts me wherever I go. I love you. I need you. I must have you."

"Wait a minute. You're insane! In fantasy it would be marvelous to marry you, but in reality it's not as easy as you think. Oh, merde! What I'm trying to say is: I need time."

"Time, you say? Time for what? Time is something I don't have plenty of, so I must let the pendulum swing in my direction. I beg you to marry me now, for tomorrow is a promissory note."

"I wish I could. But I simply cannot marry you now. That's not saying I'm closing the door for good either," I replied with all the compassion I could muster.

"Summer . . . please tell me if I'm mistaken. I have a strange feeling in my heart that tells me you love me, too."

" . . . Perhaps your heart is right. I have very strong feelings for you. Someday, in the future, when I clear my closet of old skeletons, I might consider marriage. Until then let's just be friends."

"Fou que je suis, I will wait for you till hell freezes over. You're already a part of my destiny."

"Destiny . . . what destiny? I'm beginning to loathe the sound of that word. And please don't say it was a Mouse Oracle that told you that."

"I don't know what the devil you're talking about. Honestly I don't. What is this Mouse Oracle, anyway? Is it something I should know?"

"The Mouse Oracle itself is an urn. But the mice that inhabit it are the ones that told me about my destiny's ways. Because of them I'm here. I'm a living proof of their powers."

"I still don't get it. It sounds like a story with links of sand."

Mercifully the waiter reappeared with a fresh plate of cakes and drew Salih into a weird conversation about wolves in the wild.

That afternoon at the Marquis I almost lost the entire house of the bright-faced cards. If that had happened, the result would have been as devastating as Humpty Dumpty's fall.

To me writing always meant expressing my deep thoughts concealed in small boxes deep in my heart. Since I felt ashamed of not telling the truth to Salih about my other life, I wrote a letter to myself. It sounded crazy but I had to tell someone just how much I hated the memory of my incestuous relationship and wanted to set things straight with Salih, who until now had heard me speaking with a forked tongue.

That night, despite the soothing sound of the waves lapping the shore, sleep eluded me as if I were a leper with scaly scabs. I tried to chase away the demons boring holes in my brain with an aromatic bubble bath.

Later, as I lay in the darkness, not quite sure what I should do, I fell into a strange dream in which I saw my body slowly disappearing and becoming a part of something bigger and more wonderful than my mortal self. As I drifted in and out of this twilight zone, I became aware that my head was the Mountain of the East, my stomach the Mountain of the Center, my right arm the Mountain of the North, my left arm the Mountain of the South, and my feet that of the West—like phan-Ku in Chinese mythology.

It was such a relief to see morning come wrapped in a bluish haze. By then the cobwebs in my head had begun to clear. I asked myself: now that I was caught up between two men—one as comfortable as an old slipper and the other as exciting as a ski run down a steep mountain—what should I do? Suicide was the first thing that came to mind, thereby making it easier for all. "Death is the doctor of the desperate," wrote Ramon de la Cruz y Cano. But wait, I couldn't do that. Today I was having lunch with Salih at Chez Pelikan.

Now about the truth behind the truth.

My primary reason for meeting Salih at Chez Pelikan was: the book. *Espane*—legend—was the sort of book I needed to put my own *Oratory of the Legends* over the top and all the way to the best-sellers list. *Espane* was written and illustrated by Salih's Grandmother Yildiz, who secretly had aspired to be a writer during an era when women weren't allowed to express their own personal desires. Originally the book was published in Arabic script. Later it was released in Roman characters to attract a new generation of readers who had cut their teeth on the new alphabet.

I arrived to Chez Pelikan at noon under a sizzling August sun. The restaurant, trying to create a cooling draft, had all its fans whirling faster than the famous Whirling Dervishes. The colder air flowing outside was causing passersby to jam the sidewalk—already overrun with all sorts of street vendors hawking postcards, cheap trinkets and halkas stacked on bamboo stems.

As for me, I was comfortable in a cool cotton dress with a scoop neckline, a Parisian number that a modiste in Pera had copied for me in her back-alley atelier. Without sounding vain, I must confess that I looked like a study in chic, with my hair drawn back with tiny yellow roses. As I passed a mirror, I laughed at my eye-catching reflection, remembering the time when I had shocked Uncle Hugh with my naughty entrance, wearing nothing but the skin I was born in.

However, that was yesterday's fantasy.

Today is reality. Please hear me out until I finish telling you about Appreciation. There is no place called Appreciation. Appreciation is a state of mind. You cannot go there without your imagination. And it means different things to different women. To a woman in love those twelve letters are like a beautiful rhapsody, in which she sees herself as desirable as Napoleon's Josephine, or as Lord Byron's lovely Countess Guiccioli, or Beethoven's Beloved Immortal. But, above all, she sees herself like the beautiful wife of Shah Jehan, for whom the Taj Mahal in India was built.

Now it's up to you who you want to be.

As for me, I've been to Appreciation several times. There are pictures in my scrapbook of me going there. But how did I get there in the first place? Aren't you dying to know. So let me fill you in about the time when Salih gave me a blue sapphire necklace. Appreciation was written all over it. Now that's what I mean about Appreciation, a gift for the sheer pleasure of a woman's friendship. With a hundred thousand dollars a year for spending money, when a dollar bought you a wonderful meal, I could have easily bought the necklace for myself. But, you see, it wouldn't have meant anything. And it wouldn't have taken me to Appreciation.

Tears rose in Salih's eyes when he put the necklace around my neck and saw the happiness he had given me. He could not control the joy in his voice as he told me how much he appreciated the fact that he had found his soul mate in me.

"Bey Effendi...hmmmm...perhaps you're ready to order now?" a waiter asked, approaching us almost awkwardly, too afraid to burst the bubble we were in.

"Absolutely," Salih responded and turned to me. "What do you think? Are you hungry?"

"How can I be hungry at a time like this? My happiness doesn't leave much room for food. Maybe if I force myself, I might be able to eat a bite or two."

"Bey Effendi, with all due respect, may I suggest the brochette a la Pelikan. Each succulent morsel of the swordfish is to die for. Trust me," the waiter rhapsodized as if he were the grand chef wearing an eighteen-inch high toque blanche on his head.

"Your suggestion is excellent. Swordfish happens to be one of my favorite fishes," Salih said and looked at me, trying to analyze the faraway look in my eyes. "Well...what do you think, Summer?"

"Swordfish sounds ideal."

The waiter, happy with our order, shooed the flies and displayed a crocodilian smile with protruding teeth.

A moment later, a youngish sommelier matched our swordfish with a bottle of Creusa, a drinkable work of art from Crete. Now we knew we were in for a big treat.

(An interesting footnote: Despite the fact that the Koran forbids spirits of any kind, many Muslims consume alcohol in bottles with consumer-friendly labels.)

After a few glasses of wine, Salih, in a rare mood of abandon, blurted out, "Summer, would you like to know what it has been like to be an Ottoman Prince?"

The question, so boldly put, took me off guard.

"Only if it isn't too painful for you," I responded calmly, trying to keep my excitement in check.

"To be honest, nowadays I prefer not to weigh myself down with the nostalgia of discarded memories. Life is more bearable that way. But . . . now and then I like to tell a few juicy tidbits to get a rise out of people. You know, it's no fun to keep memories in my comfort zone forever," Salih continued and dropped his eyelids as though he needed a few private minutes to pore over the pages of his childhood diary, hidden in God's little library.

"Salih, I must be truthful with you. Whatever you say might end up as food for my readers. Do you have any problems with that?"

"Of course not. The way I see it, sooner or later the whole world will know who were God's Vice Regents on earth, and hear all the horrid details of their cruelty and debauchery."

"Are you completely sure?"

"Yes."

"Okay. Let's move along, then."

"First, let me tell you what I feared the most: The silken bowstring. The terror of the silken bowstring controlled every aspect of my life. Growing up in the Yildiz Palace was like living in a dungeon with crystal chandeliers. In those days, I only had one friend that I could count on. It was the piano. My passion for the piano was a great joke to the harem women. No one could understand this passion, except my father. Because he, too, loved the piano as much as I did. It's no secret that my father had hundreds of pianos scattered all through the palace; some were used for playing and others as decorative barriers.

"A host of well-meaning servants did their best to protect me from palace ridicule. I found great comfort in the memory of my Uncle, Sultan Abdul Aziz, who himself was devoted to the piano. In fact, the historians tell us that Sultan Abdul Aziz used to strap pianos to men's backs, insisting that a pianist play while he strolled through the palace gardens."

"Salih...isn't it amazing how some of us get so wrapped up in things we love? Look at me. I'm living proof that in order to achieve happiness, I must bury myself in writing."

"But wait, there is more," Salih said. "You see, I was not a child prodigy, let alone a musical savant. Plain and simple. I needed a piano teacher who could help me to see the real talent in me. For the first time in my life I was happy, because of Roger van der Zelt, my Flemish piano teacher, who was hired to whip me into shape. He was allowed into the palace because he was blind, and not a threat to the harem. Speaking of the harem, let me tell you that the harem was guarded by Kisler Aga, the Chief Black Eunuch, and his retinue of castrated black eunuchs, who were brought from Africa. They all belonged to the same color group: dark black."

"Are you still in touch with Monsieur van der Zelt?"

"Of course. Matter of fact, he married one of my father's Circassian odalisques, after the harem was abolished and Father was deported to Salonika. Despite his handicap, he used to brag that he could clearly see his wife's face in his mind's eye. He absolutely adored her."

"Ahhhh! The power of love."

This conversation, though fascinating was beginning to wear on me. I was dying to be guided on another path between the pages of history. In other words, to hear about the bizarre practices and other degrading acts that went on behind the palace walls. Talk about nerve! The timing couldn't have been better to ask Salih about this aspect of palace life.

"Salih...hmmmm...is it true that one of your uncles, I cannot remember his name, used to sear the women's breasts with a hot iron just to boost his ego? Can this be true?" I asked, fighting the goose bumps forming on top of my head.

"Sadly, it's true. It was Sultan Mahomet the Third. He committed many such cruel acts, mostly aimed at women, because of his uncontrollable temper.

"Now I have something more intimate to tell you. Once, when I was a boy of twelve, I peed on the head of a red-haired girl, for no other reason than I was angry at her. That's my sole claim to fame."

"That's it?"

"Well, what did you expect? I'm sorry that I failed to rise to your expectation."

"Well...I think that's hilarious. I admire your twisted sense of humor."

The restaurant was now rather full. In the midst of all the laughter and clinking glasses, Salih and I shared a deafening silence. I could feel it pressing against my eardrums. I took a quick look at Salih. He seemed totally happy to be in a dreamlike state. Then, in perfect style, he smiled and said, "Summer, I have saved the best for the last.

"According to my father, Sultan Mohamet's decadent behavior was nothing compared with Sultan Ibrahim's grotesque acts of debauchery. No amount of imagination could ever compare with what I'm about to tell you. I'm warning you, it's bad. I hope you can stomach it. When Ibrahim was in his twenties with raging hormones, he would strip naked the prettiest of his concubines and make them pretend that they were beautiful mares in heat. Then he ran among them, squealing like a stallion, banging one after the other, as long as his stamina would bear."

"Wow! He must have been some man."

"And with a tremendous sexual appetite, to say the least."

"Come to think of it, weren't there any laws to protect women from such macabre acts?"

"My dear girl, I'm talking about a period in Ottoman history, when a Sultan considered himself to be God's Shadow on earth, thus a man above all other men, and free to do as he pleased."

"Salih, it all seems so utterly ogrish. On second thought, what about human rights?" I asked. This disturbing thought brought a bad case of the jitters, for I already knew the answer to my question.

"Human rights? Now that's funny. Because in those days human rights were two words that seldom reached a Sultan's ears. No one dared to approach such matters with the Sultan. That's how things were then. And, perhaps we should take a few minutes to talk about your own Negro slaves, who were also subjected to inhuman treatment by their white masters. Do you ever stop to think about that? Now let's see what you have to say."

"That's a sad chapter in the American history, something that doesn't make me very proud," I replied, realizing how inadequate my words were.

"How very clever of you to brush off the subject so gracefully."

"Oh, Salih, I'm so sorry. But I don't know what to say."

"Just say that you love me, despite my family's dark past."

"That I can do. I love you Salih, for you are a gentle man with a touch of magic."

"Please don't stop," he begged me.

"Okay. Also you are handsome and entitled to a woman who can light up your life . . . much better than I can."

"Sometimes you act like you don't have the slightest

notion of your effect on me," Salih whispered in my ear.

I took a deep breath and said, "Yes, I do. But this is not a good time to go into it."

A sad look glazed Salih's dark eyes. He stared at me without uttering a single word. But by the time the coffee was served, he was talking animatedly and apologized for his lack of understanding.

"I promised you a book. So, here it is. It's an interesting piece of work. Because, you see, my grandmother's wit was legendary."

"I don't know how to thank you. On the other hand, I do. See what I have for you," I exclaimed and blushed. The gift in question was a small replica of the Golden Gate Bridge, in San Francisco, wrought in gold and platinum. I had ordered it from Cartier.

"How exquisitely beautiful. You're spoiling me. This is a gift that I will cherish far beyond the grave. And I will see that it doesn't end in the Armenian Victory Museum."

"I'm happy that I was able to make you happy. I was determined to give you a small trinket that would remind you of me."

"Oh, Summer—this precious gift can never be a substitute for your hand in marriage. I adore you! You stir my blood with wild desire. Please, don't torment me, just say you'll marry me."

"Salih, I must congratulate you for saying the sweetest things. Unfortunately, the answer is still no."

"What's wrong with marriage? Pray tell me."

"There is nothing wrong with marriage, per se. The problem is me. I'm not quite ready for such a big commitment."

"As for me, I will not rest until I put a ring on your finger."

"Well . . . maybe some day you will."

"I'm a patient man. I can wait."

"Please understand that I'm not against love and marriage. But before I can make such a big leap, first I have to put my house in order. There are just too many skeletons in my closet. I hope you know what I mean."

"I think so. We all have our own personal demons to deal with."

Then in a burst of love, I wanted to kiss him, to caress him, to shower him with sweet words. Yet, I couldn't let myself deceive him. I respected him too much for that. *How can I tell this man, who thinks I'm virginal white, that I am leading a double life? It would be violating all sense of decency.*

It's easy to see why suddenly Salih decided on a change of venue.

"Summer . . . I have a wonderful idea. Let's get away from all this talk of marriage and palace ghosts. We can rent a boat, fitted with silk carpets, velvet pillows and blankets made of the finest Bursa silk, and drift out to sea—like Loti and Aziyade in the throes of love. Well . . . ?"

"Whoa, Nelly! I believe you're pushing the bar a bit too high for me. You can't be serious. Or are you?"

"I'm dead serious."

"I'm afraid you've read a few too many novels. Because what you're suggesting is a scene right out of Loti's imagination. In a fantasy world all is possible. But in the real world things just don't always happen as planned."

"Come on, Summer . . . where is your sense of adventure?"

"At the present time, my sense of adventure is in a dormant state, but speaking of Loti, how would you like to take me to the cemetery where Aziyade is buried? I believe the cemetery is somewhere in Topkapi. I'd like to take a few snapshots of Aziyade's headstone for a story I'm doing on harem women."

"Did I ever tell you about the time when I met the Great Seducer, as he was referred to then? Loti came to Yildiz Palace; my father was fond of him. It was sometime in August of 1913. As for taking you to the cemetery, it will be my pleasure. However, let's make it soon. Because of reasons beyond my control, I have to return to Paris by the end of the month."

"I don't mean to pry, but do the Armenians have anything to do with your sudden departure?"

"Sort of. It's best that we not discuss it. Security, you know."

"I'm sorry, I didn't mean any harm."

"I know that. Summer, come to Paris with me! You can write there just as easily as you do here. Let's do something crazy—like getting married in a carriage in the Bois de Boulogne. Well . . . what do you say?"

"I say you are crazy. You know that's impossible."

"Here we go again. Dead on the track, before we even start."

"That's the way it's got to be, at least for now. But how about a rain check?"

And so we parted.

By then the daylight was holding hands with twilight. The entire city looked like a giant electric bulb, waiting for the night-people to come out. As I walked, a certain aubergine suit in a shop window caught my attention. The suit's exquisite cut and color were an ode to French couture. And it would be the perfect color to wear to the cemetery—when the entire extent of the silent park would be taken over by the purple daisy and amethyst foxglove.

118

13

Two men look out through the same bars.
One sees mud, and the other one the stars.
                                        —F. Langbridge

It began innocently enough. One Saturday evening my friend, Sevim Alaz, an author best known for her children's books, gave a dinner party at her family's yali on the Bosphorus. That evening was the beginning of my friendship with Teyze Jale, Sevim's grand-aunt, who lived in a wooden mansion in Uskudar, next door to a fortuneteller who was an authority on foretelling the future.

So entranced were we by Teyze Jale's stories that we decided to call on Leyla Hanim, the fortuneteller.

If symbolism can speak a thousand words, consider that the first impression was a pleasant one. Leyla Hanim's house, nestled among ancient boulders and curtained with wisteria and honeysuckle, was anything but scary. In fact it was comfortable and homey. To my surprise there were no gargoyles peering down from the rooftops, nor cobwebs spun across an eerie black door. Despite its romantic past, the house with its missing sideboards, was in a state of despair.

We walked up a short gravel drive, overhung with mulberry and fig trees that abruptly ended at the front door. It was decorated with aromatic swags of native flowers and herbs, a pleasant touch that put us at ease almost immediately.

The best, though, was yet to come.

Suddenly, the door screeched on its rusty hinges and opened wide, revealing a woman with a semi-transparent silk scarf across the lower part of her face. I was bowled over as I had never been before.

"Please enter," Leyla Hanim said, in a well-rehearsed tone of voice. She offered us little red velvet chairs, typical of the wellborn of that era. She herself sat on a small divan, draped with a fine Turkish carpet with matching pillows and rocked her torso back and forth with eyes shut and lips moving. It seemed as though she was making her way through another dimension. This strange act went on for some indefinite time. There was little that we could do but wait and listen to the buzzing insects.

At last things began to happen.

"Kizim—daughter—my spirit guide, Nazan, tells me a certain venture isn't as far fetched as previously thought. Follow the present path a little further and success will be there waiting for you. The next few months will be tumultuous, and perhaps you will need a tot or two of whiskey before this is over. But don't worry. Kismet is about to allow you a second chance. Grasp it with both hands," Leyla Hanim said, and rubbed together her henna-dyed fingers. "Waffle now and you'll sink like a stone. It's best to be on guard. Now . . . listen, and listen well. In the city of the Sultans there is a man, I believe a Muslim, who has fallen in love with you. It may be very shocking to think that this man in question is marked for death," Leyla Hanim continued and walked to the window to admire the peacocks strolling in her garden.

"Leyla Hanim, it is very important that you tell me everything you see in your vision. Is the man tall or short? Does he have heavy-lidded dark eyes? Is his hair thick and black? You know, the sort of things a woman likes to know."

"Kizim . . . don't worry. Everything about this man is perfect. There is, however, a fly in the soup. It's ugly and it might break your heart."

"Now I'm worried. What is it?"

"I see in the shadows a man. I believe a Christian, for he is wearing a cross around his neck. He is pointing a gun. There is something very disturbing about this man," she commented and sank into the sofa to smoke a cigarette.

I was almost sure the man holding the gun was the Armenian assassin, a shifty-eyed opportunist who struck suddenly.

Leyla Hanim took several deeps puffs from her cigarette and closed her eyes. She appeared to be in communication with her spirit guide. Then she made a ninety-degree turn to face Sevim.

"Kucuk Kizim . . . *iyi bir haber*—good news—after months of chasing mirages, you've found what you've been searching for. Now be happy and don't let anything or anyone get in your way. Remain positive and the fish will jump into your net. I see marriage. The man has a formidable wealth. Also I see children, two boys and twin girls. *Masallah*! Kizim, you're lucky," the seeress remarked.

"Twin girls . . . Did you really see them?"

"I saw them as clearly as I was allowed to see. At times the vision was a little murky, but I have no doubt that I saw them."

"Ohhh! I'm so happy. This wasn't the way I had envisioned my future. To be honest, it's hundred times better. *Cok tesekkur ederim*—thank you very much," Sevim cooed and hugged herself as though to protect herself from a falling star that might land on her and remove her dreams to the land of charred hopes.

"Kizim . . . I want you to know that the father of your children is a doctor and handsome to boot," Leyla Hanim added with a broad smile.

"And the wedding?"

"I wish I knew," Leyla Hanim answered and went stone quiet. Perhaps she saw no reason to discuss at length the details of the wedding. But from the look of things, it was apparent she was expecting someone important and was anxious to end the session, and get us out of the house. You could almost feel, taste and hear the state of her anxiety, for she scraped the edge of the wooden table with her fingernails like a large cat sharpening its claws.

Shortly after that, Leyla Hanim escorted us into a dim parlor, scented with attar of roses. The windows were hung with faded blue-slate satin drapes; no elegant decorations these, but the tattered garments worn by a house that had seen the better days of the Ottoman Empire. Equally impressive but old was a red velvet *fauteuil*, supporting a picture framed with gilt wood. What an odd way to display a photograph!

In a sudden burst of emotion, Leyla Hanim literally jumped out of her skin and took on a strange persona. Speaking in Turkish, but with a heavy Anatolian dialect, she blurted out, while tears cascaded down her face as she pointed to the picture on the chair, "How dare you turn your back on Sultan Abdul Aziz, God's Shadow on Earth?" I turned around to see to whom she was talking. There was no one in the room but us and a silky-furred Angora cat that meowed continuously and rubbed itself against my legs.

"You infidels have little or no regard for our Ottoman

Sultans, isn't that so? Don't you know that one must always face a Sultan, whether coming or leaving?" she asked, her eyes oozing with disgust.

For a minute or two I thought this must be a bad joke. But she seemed dead serious. Her weird behavior made me wonder what causes someone to attach such profound meaning to a mere photograph.

But Leyla Hanim's strange behavior made me take a few steps backward to glance again at the photograph of Sultan Abdul Aziz and look for an expression of some sort—because in 1876, he had committed suicide by severing his arteries with a pair of scissors.

"I want you to know that Sultan Abdul Aziz and four of his favorite odalisques come to my house almost every afternoon. They love my delicious *kurabiyes*," Leyla Hanim said, arranging and rearranging a plateful of stale-looking cookies on the table. "Listen...hush! Can you hear the *clip-clops* of horses' hooves on the cobbles? You must leave at once," she added with perfect composure as if she were talking about an imminent disaster, rather than something that might have occurred eons ago when her ancestors lived in the house.

It appeared that we were dealing with a woman with a psychiatric disorder who had one foot in the past and one foot in the present. For whatever reason, she had momentarily lost all touch with reality and seemed perfectly happy in the company of phantoms of years past.

By the time we were ready to leave, Leyla Hanim had re-transported herself from the past to the present, from fantasy to reality and from delusion to truth. She laughed and carried on as though nothing strange had taken place within these walls. She asked us whether we were happy with our fortunes, and expressed concern for our trip back to San Stefano.

On that moonless evening, as we made our way through ghostly cypress trees toward the harbor, we imagined all sorts of goblins playing hide-and-seek in the shadows of the tall trees. According to a legend, everyone was safe in Uskudar, because the village was protected by a fire-breathing sea creature that would emerge from the water to strike down any evil. Despite the comforting language of the myth, it fell short of attaining our full confidence on that pitch dark night filled with the noiseless flights of the flat-faced owls.

14

I cannot with thee live, nor yet without thee.
—Martial

That glorious May, I was bursting with energy and high hopes, partly because it was spring, partly because Salih was taking me to Eyup, roughly sixty miles (as the crow flies) from Galata Bridge.

Though Salih regarded Eyup—after Mecca, Medina and Jerusalem—as the most holy ground in Orthodox Islam, I was a little sensitive about the entire subject because I knew so little about that neck of the woods. Of course the highlight of the trip was to be the tomb of Eyup Ansari, the standard bearer of Prophet Mohammed, and the Eyup Ansari Mosque in Eyup.

It might as well be said that the Golden Horn in the spring is like viewing a private jewelry collection by a skilled artist.

The taxi deposited us at the Galata Bridge just as the captain of the ferryboat clanged the bell. Our fellow travelers were, for the most part, men—men in drab, dark clothes, or dressed in long robes of white homespun with flowing sleeves, their heads covered with white turbans. A few women enveloped in black, billowy dresses, their necks adorned with gold-coin necklaces, sat close together in quiet melancholy, chewing mastic with a surprising show of gold teeth.

The women observed us with the kohl-lined eyes.

The intensity of their glare perhaps had something to do with the fascination the Turks have with foreigners and their laissez-faire life style. But mostly because I was a *gavur*, an infidel, on a ferry headed for Eyup, the most sacred quarter of Constantinople—where Christians were tolerated as being only a notch above dogs. Hmmmm . . . on second thought, why should a gavur be so disliked by Muslims? Do you know?

Probably not.

As the ferry advanced up the inlet under a freshly polished blue sky, each slap of the waves seemed to speak both of the past and the present in the most bizarre way. In a sudden flight of fantasy, I saw myself traveling with Byzas, the Greek adventurer, who had sailed these waters in the seventh century B.C. It is more than possible that Byzas fell in love with the Golden Horn and, thinking he had found Paradise, went on to build the city of Byzantium. But, like many other best laid plans, this too would soon go awry.

However, to fully understand the extent of Byzas' passion, one must travel the back roads of his mind and listen to the distant echoes of his heartbeat. Like all those who dream of running off to an unspoiled paradise, Byzas wasn't the first man to be overtaken by the strength of such a fantasy. That notion has beguiled dreamers from Odysseus and Prospero to the Swiss Family Robinson.

At the head of the Golden Horn (also known as the Sweet Waters of Europe), lay Eyup under a fine mist of rain. Its quiet beauty aroused in me an emotion which fell just short of tears; in it affection, sadness and pride are combined. According to Boris, a man incapable of responding to beauty with *umilenie*, is dead to the world.

I smiled broadly as I caught sight of Pierre Loti's

house beside the landing stage now mummified in a red-colored vine. It boasted an air of utter arrogance almost daring one not to like it, not to go near it.

Somewhere deep in your heart you want to believe that Loti was at his happiest in Eyup, surrounded by Aziyade's youthful energy. After all she was only sixteen, which made Loti oblivious to the passing of the years. It is again possible to see Loti as a man, who cringed at the thought of aging, a time when the flesh cries in distress. Many years later Loti confessed that only two things were important in life: youth and sun.

That said, all that stood between Loti's house and the Eyup Ansari Mosque was a grass-grown street.

I felt a wonderful sense of peace and exaltation when we entered the mosque and stood under its hemispherical dome. Caught up in this feeling of great joy I sensed the presence of souls in limbo, who were passing through the mosque on their way to Heaven. But that is, as they say, another story for another time.

Beside the traveling spirits, a few pilgrims were on their hands and knees on thick carpets, communicating in silent prayers with Eyup, who was buried in a marble tomb encased with silver. Nearby on a table, covered with a crimson cloth, lay the Prophet's sword, its golden hilt encrusted with precious stones. According to Eyup's own legend, he was assigned to carry the Prophet's sword, because he possessed the quality of soul that cannot be bought or sold. It made me even more joyfully humble when I thought I heard Eyup's voice in my head. *There is no God but God, and I bear witness that Mohammed is His slave and His Prophet.*

That day Eyup's wise words altered the color of my soul.

I recorded all these experiences in my journal nearly

half a century ago. Today as then, they are as fresh and as true as when I wrote them.

Never in the world, except in San Francisco, have I seen anything to equal the beauty of Princess Ummi's crumbling summerhouse. Its stone walls were layered with yellow honeysuckle, white jasmine and threaded with small pink roses. It is still a mystery as to why the lovely princess chose this flower-trimmed valley to build such an awesome house.

According to one legend (the exact story varies widely, depending on who is recounting it) the princess wanted to create a special place to share with nightingales, where she and her innamorato could meet and make love without being detected.

For the next thirty minutes Salih and I walked and picked wildflowers. This was not unusual, because the fertile valley abounded with red poppies and bluebells. Suddenly, Salih came to a dead stop and whispered into my ear, "Listen."

"What am I listening to?" I asked.

"Nightingales," Salih answered, pointing to a distant orchard.

"Where are they? Are they in the almond trees?"

"Almond trees and apricot trees."

"I cannot see them. There are acres of trees."

"I tell you . . . they are out there. Just keep listening and watching. Sooner or later you'll spot one."

"I thought nightingales, especially the males, sang at night and only during breeding season."

"Yes, that's true. It just goes to show you what a male has to do in order to attract a female."

"Well . . . isn't that true of all the species?"

In the midst of the ongoing nightingale duel, a sudden sparrow chorus brought to mind a story that I heard in San Francisco. I decided to share it with Salih.

"Salih...I have a story to tell you. Once a woman wins a contest. When she is asked how she intends to spend her prize money, she giggles happily and replies, 'A fruit orchard in California to feed my body and a bird farm in Florida to feed my soul.' I think it's so sweet."

"Now that you brought it up," Salih said, "I have a bird story for you, too. When I was four or five, I found a tiny sparrow fluttering in one of the dark corridors in Yildiz. As the days continued, I found myself obsessed with the bird. I nurtured and loved it, but it died. I buried it secretly under the mulberry tree growing outside my window. I'm sure it's still there, at least its ghost is, for I felt its body beside me for the longest time."

"Strangely enough I had a similar experience, but with a dog. I cried endlessly when Joy, my beloved Doberman, died. I still keep her picture on my dresser. It reminds me that once I loved the perfect dog."

"It's a good story, Summer. Cherish the memory."

"Salih, obviously you're a nature lover. Tell me... have you ever been on a picnic?"

"Is this leading to another story?"

"No, not really."

"Listen...one of these days we'll have an American-style picnic with fried chicken, potato salad, corn on the cob and apple pie. That's as American as it gets. Okay?"

"Before I say yes, let me ask you... can you cook?"

"Of course I can cook. I've been told by those in the know, that they've never tasted fried chicken to rival my own! But it was not always so. I recall the time when I forgot to put shortening in my piecrust. The dough was so hard you needed a hammer to break open the pie, literally. That year I was the butt of all the jokes. But that didn't stop me from trying to make a better piecrust."

"Thank you for warning me. But that's not saying I won't eat your pies."

"I believe my confession lost me my star status, at least in your eyes."

"Hell no! As for me, I can barely boil water; I'm all thumbs when it comes to cooking."

"Well, that's a relief. I'm glad you're not perfect."

"After all is said and done, who cares whether you can cook or not? What really matters to me is our friendship. When I saw you for the first time in Pomme d'Or looking so bewitchingly attractive, I knew kismet had brought us together."

"You say kismet and I say destiny."

"Kismet always knows when two people are meant for each other."

"I sure hope this isn't leading to where I think it's leading."

"No, don't worry. I'm not going to ask you to marry me today. Maybe tomorrow, or the next day, but not today."

That said, he managed a small smile and grabbed my hand and pulled me after him down a hill and up another. "Now, Summer, where would you like to go first? Café Pierre Loti, or the park of the Weeping Willows?"

"I prefer Café Pierre Loti," I replied, not certain why I had chosen the café over the park.

Best scene: bright-faced white flowers growing between red pantiles and rotting bird carcasses on the roof of the Café Loti.

The second best scene: a mouse. Perhaps a mouse isn't chic enough to talk about—but on the other hand, what is chic or unchic in a place like this—where the clients looked as unchic as the mouse? For the most part, the habitués were young intellectuals caged in their own moment. Several tables were taken by small groups of tanned and lean individuals, who seemed to be in some sort of twilight zone. They sat in rigid calmness, hoping to catch a glimpse of Loti's ghost, dressed in a Turkish costume. For the fashionable rich the café was a good place to explore new avenues of paranormal—when such beliefs were meaningful during the flamboyant era of oracles and mystics.

As for the mouse, this was no ordinary rodent. It was the sanitized contemporary version of the familiar barn mouse we're all familiar with. This cute beastie was shiny gray, holding a piece of bread in its mouth. In my imagination's borderless scope, it was easy to imagine that the mouse I saw was Pierre Loti in one of his bizarre guises. At one point, the sound of the moving chairs scared the shy rodent and it ran across the stone terrace and into a hole in the wall—no bigger than the tip of a thumb. A few minutes later the mouse came out again, sniffed the air and went back into its hole.

"Summer . . . knock, knock . . . hello . . . is anybody home?"

"I'm terribly sorry. I didn't mean to ignore you. Absurd as it may sound, I was watching a mouse that resembled Loti—minus all the paint, rouge and powder that Loti used when in disguise. Honestly, I'm not making this up."

"Hmmmm . . . a mouse . . . you say?"

"Yes, a mouse. I'm telling you—or at least I'm trying to tell you that what I saw was Loti disguised as a mouse. Does that make any sense to you?"

"Okay, okay, I believe you."

"That's better. I knew you would understand—once you put your mind to it."

The weather was unseasonably warm that spring. After a short pause to quench our thirst, what I found even more curious was Salih's puzzled expression looking for ways to tell the truth without hurting my feelings.

"Summer as you know—Loti died on June 10, 1923. He was buried in a very deep grave in Oleron, France. Therefore, why would he want to return to Eyup to pretend to be a mouse? It just is too hilarious for words."

"As far as I'm concerned, there are two schools of thought: one, to regain his Oriental life. And second, to be reunited with Aziyade. After all, there is something magical about the power of love."

"I still say, Loti was much too elegant to appear as a mouse. But stranger things have happened in the world."

"I've always been very curious about the capability of the spirit—once it leaves its shell. Where does it go? To me that's just the biggest mystery of all the ages."

"To be honest, I never took the time to ask the spirits where they were headed. As for Loti, he was a wolf, but a charmingly romantic wolf with consistency of style. To this day, women adore him and wish their husbands were more like him—romantic, gentle, generous, blood tinglingly sexy. And to the men Loti is the image of all they longed to be—hypnotic, talented, and a master of seduction. Without a doubt, Loti was one of a vanishing species."

"Salih, please continue. I love the eloquence of your well-chosen words describing Loti."

"Actually, I can do better than that. Here read this book—*Aziyade*—written by Loti in 1876, when he was at the zenith of his romanticism. *Aziyade* is a story of love and despair written at a time when a harem woman wouldn't have dreamed of having an extramarital affair with a man, let alone a gavur Frenchman."

"To my way of thinking, I'm sure it was the boredom of the harem life that pushed Aziyade over the edge. For God's sake! She was only sixteen with teenage fantasies. I can well understand her anxieties."

"Perhaps you are right. Chekov reminds us that people who lead lonely existences always have something on their minds that they are eager to talk about. Therefore, it's fair to assume that Loti became the theatre for all Aziyade's dreams, and her only escape from the doldrums of everyday life," Salih said, and took a sip of his coffee.

"As it happens to all good things—the floating bed, the silk pillows, the thick carpets, the mystery of Eyup, the luxury of the Oriental life—all vanished in a single huff, because Loti no longer had a place for Aziyade in his Catholic upbringing. He returned to France to marry a French Protestant girl, and that put an end to the good thing he once had," Salih said and breathed a sigh of relief.

"Salih, do you suppose Loti walked away from Aziyade because he was a gavur, an uncircumcised Christian dog, not worthy of Islam? The Koran is specific on hospitality. But there is no denying that there exists an invisible dividing line between the Christians and the Muslims," I said flatly, wondering about Salih's reaction to my comment. Of course, I could have sugar-coated the question of the "Christian dog" and said an "infidel," which would have been more proper, I suppose. But the way I saw it, why corrupt words in the face of reality?

"Well, my dear, don't be ridiculous. What you just said isn't entirely true. You could not have possibly known that in the sixteenth century Suleyman the Magnificent married Roxalana, the red-haired daughter of a Russian priest. My own grandmother was an Armenian dancer before entering Sultan Majid's harem. And we must not forget Flora Corbier, a Belgian modiste, who was my father's paramour. As I grew into adulthood, there were many times when I wondered why my father, who had two hundred concubines in his harem in Yildiz, preferred the company of a Christian woman? And according to the palace *dedikodu* (gossip) Flora gave birth to a girl, sired by my father, though he never acknowledged her as his," Salih explained and reached into his pocket to retrieve a small golden locket. "Here is my half-sister, Menekse, Flora's child. Look at her, isn't she simply adorable?" Salih asked as he opened the locket.

"True, true, she is beautiful. Whatever happened to her?"

"Do you really want to know? I warn you the answer will shock you," he replied, never taking his eyes off me.

"Bear in mind that I'm a writer, and a writer is always looking for an interesting story to capture on paper. Without people like you, *The Oratory of the Legends* would have withered and died, before I could realize my dream."

"Poor Menekse. She lies somewhere on the bottom of the sea with the rest of the unwanted harem women."

"But why?"

"Good question. Yet I can't answer it. Only my father knows why, and he isn't talking. Even Menekse's devoted slaves couldn't save her from her fate. Fortunately for Father, no one talked against him. So her death became just a whisper in the wind. After her death, one of the slave women gave me her diary. Would you like to read it?"

"Of course I would! You are an angel."

"I'm not an angel, yet. But I hope to be someday. However, the diary comes with a steep price."

"Since when do we put unreasonably high price tags

on those important elements: love and friendship?"

"As I've already said, I'm no angel...could this be your way of bargaining for better terms for the diary?"

"Well...it's certainly a thought. What is it that you want from me?"

"The price tag in question is a blank card. It allows me to fill in any amount, as the occasion calls for. It has nothing to do with money. In short: I want you to kiss me tonight, here on the ferry."

"Well...would you settle for a friendly hug? And no pleadings for my hand?"

When that failed to elicit a response, I said, "Speaking of the hand and other such entrapments, please tell me with how many wives must I share you?"

"None. Ours will be a monogamous union. I will love you and only you forever."

"And when I'm old, wrinkled and strewn with ugly age spots, and you cannot bear the sight of me, are you going to toss me into the sea, like your father used to do?"

"Never. In the words of Shakespeare: To me, fair lady, you never can be old."

"Continuing along in a similar vein, let me say I think that Byron had me in mind when he wrote: The wandering outlaws of his dark mind."

"In Islam we believe that only Allah can achieve perfection. It is a deadly sin to try to compete with Allah! Yet I, in my own humble way, have succeeded in capturing the love of a woman as exquisite as you. Now I'm a hopeless romantic who needs to marry you."

"I say, give me time to meditate on it."

"I'm sure in time I will win you over."

As soon as the ferry departed, Salih and I sat down on a leather-covered bench near the bow on the portside. The night was so mesmerically soft that I feared I might have to bribe some jealous gods for it. I recall the way I smiled as I watched the lights of Eyup slowly melt into the darkness as though wanting to make way for the stars yet to come.

Suddenly, at the slap of a large wave, Salih's body fell against mine, his face on my face and his arms wrapped around my waist. This was too close for comfort, yet it aroused in me an erotic feeling which made my head spin. I had no choice but to push him away. He looked like a man going through the worst pains of love. This might be laughable if it were not so genuine.

Somewhere in the darkness, Galata bridge hung in the air like a span of gold. At the same time this visual feast was served against an architectural backdrop of mosques, golden domes, tall minarets and moon-blanched palaces centuries old.

Quite honestly, I was in a state of wonderment the rest of the night. But for the moment all that mattered was that we parted with a friendly kiss on the cheek and saying that the day had been a wonderful experience that would bring us the most happiness.

15

How else but through a broken heart
may Lord Christ enter in?
            —Oscar Wilde

Meanwhile, at the Red Poppy, Daddy was about to under-
take a mega project. He called Uncle Hugh and asked him
to return to Sonoma to oversee the expansion of the winery. This sudden request wasn't above suspicion. Because
with Daddy it's always been the first man gets the olive,
the second man gets the pit.

As I reflect on times long gone, I can see how we
totally missed the punch line of the request. There had to
be one. Come to think of it, it was all about Pierre Duggar,
a man said to have the best nose in California's wine
country. American by birth, though thoroughly French by
training, Pierre was Sonoma and Napa counties' most
sought after vineyard keeper. Pierre had befriended
Uncle Hugh when they both were newbies cutting their
teeth at Red Poppy.

Now Pierre was Daddy's object of prey.

The simple truth was, Daddy needed Pierre more
than he needed Uncle Hugh. I'm guessing, of course, but I
tend to believe bringing back Uncle Hugh was a well-
orchestrated scheme to snare Pierre from Rockcliff Winery, where Pierre had successfully tested new marketing
ideas for the wines produced at Rockcliff. Because, you
see, Pierre was the sort of man for whom wine and suc-

cess existed on the same page.

As for me, this was not the happiest of times. Uncle Hugh's departure left a huge void in my life. In my despair, I took refuge in my writing. I couldn't write fast enough. Words were obscuring the pages faster than my thoughts.

This writing pattern continued until Tearson O'Brien came to call on me. Several years before, I walked into a gallery on Elma Sokak in Constantinople, and was so entranced by the portrait of a girl with a big yellow hat, painted by an artist called Tearson O'Brien, that I commissioned a similar one (but with a blue hat), to give to Uncle Hugh as a birthday present. That chance encounter, the kind that sparks friendship, was the beginning of the attachment between us.

Tearson, an acute observer, picked up on my loneliness. Because, as she put it, all my sentences began and ended with Uncle Hugh.

"Summer . . . you look so unhappy. You need a change of scenery. Go to Prinkipo. According to those people who are famous just for being famous, Prinkipo is a dream island in the Marmara Sea with a powerful sense of the past, yet modern enough to cater to all your needs in an obscenely beautiful way."

"Oh, I don't know. I would never consider going to such a romantic place without Uncle Hugh."

"I cannot count the number of times I have gone into hiatus just to energize my creative juices. A few days of absolute silence will help you with your writing, in a constructive way."

"I suppose you're right. I promise that I will be on the first ferry tomorrow morning."

"Good girl. I will check on you in a few days. Have fun, drink in the beauty."

Without any hesitation, I turned to Boris and told him to pack a small case with a few pieces of clothing, suitable for a short stay in Prinkipo.

I smile as I remember how delighted I was with the quaint hotel and the scent of sun-baked oranges and lemons, growing luxuriantly in flower beds overrun with wide-loped petunias.

Le Pigeonnier, it was called in those days. I don't know if it still exists. Maybe by now Le Pigeonnier has passed into the realms of memory.

I arrived at the hotel as dusk closed in. The weather was ideal, almost silent. The hotel, steeped in an old world charm, had all its windows open as though wanting to let in all the perfume of pine bark and lavender. The gardens leaned a bit toward fantasy with a circle of white impatiens followed with dark grass as though made by dancing fairies.

Can you imagine my utter surprise when, in the midst of this visual banquet, visions of Clouds danced before my eyes? I really cannot say why. Because this place was everything Clouds wasn't. I squinted my eyes trying to see more clearly. It was Clouds alright. While still in the throes of fantasy, the sudden voice of a Turkish strawberry peddler made me realize I wasn't in San Francisco.

By habit, I'm a morning hawk. I love to prey on the early sun, rather than let the sun prey on me. But on that morning I allowed the golden rays of the sun to lie on my bed, while my eyes massaged the blue sky as softly as a furrier fingering a pelt. This moment of softness was captured in my memory like a lovely rose opening in its moment in summer.

Breakfast at Le Pigeonnier was impossibly heavenly. The aroma of carrot and marzipan muffins, nut-studded apricot tarts, hot cinnamon biscuits, carried to my window by the morning breeze was enough to catapult me out of my bed still dreamy-eyed, to seek the breakfast table set among cages of singing yellow canaries.

Sadly enough, the Prinkipo I once knew isn't the Prinkipo of today. The island changed a lot during the last century. Many years later, an antiquarian offered me a small book for a big price. The language was difficult. But, with the help of a translator, I was taken back to the time when Homer used to come to Prinkipo from Smyrna. One wonders what were Homer's thoughts, as he penned the verses for *Iliad* and the *Odyssey*—sustained with so much artistic expression that cost little or nothing.

Like all good things, this brief stop ended on high notes.

Three days later, like a wounded bird that stops on dry land just long enough to heal its broken wing, I too flew away on the evening ferry waiting at the harbor.

As by magic, a black butterfly, its wings heavy with a dusting of salt, landed on my left shoulder. I shrieked in terror, remembering the words of the Chinese herbalist in San Francisco's China Town. According to the herbalist, an old man thoroughly steeped in Chinese mythology, a black butterfly is almost always the reincarnation of someone dead who returns to earth to see the living. And now, this butterfly on my shoulder to spoil the remains of a happy day . . .

When I arrived at Mon Plaisir, there was a neatly folded telegram waiting for me on my desk. Immediately I let out a scream. I just *knew* that the telegram was a harbinger of bad news. I can always smell the odorless scent of trouble, however softly it travels.

The telegram was from Norman Cummings, Uncle Hugh's attorney in San Francisco, and it read: "I extend my deepest sympathy to you, my dear Summer. Hugh died in an unfortunate accident at the Red Poppy. Arriving at Constantinople on the twentieth to discuss with you the terms of Hugh's will, in which you are the sole beneficiary. Very sincerely, Norman."

The telegram struck terror to my heart. I felt light-headed with a pain that incapacitated the right side of my body. I was sure I was about to have a major stroke. A report of Uncle Hugh's death had to be a terrible mistake, for I couldn't picture him laid out cold in the ground. Then reality hit, the tears came, and I cried until I had no more tears left. Soon tears gave way to screams. "God, wherever you are, speak to me! Say that You haven't called him back. I need him here on earth. Otherwise I will hate you. God, did You hear what I just said? I said I hate you. First You took my baby and now Uncle Hugh. You keep taking and taking. You're either an all-loving, compassionate God, or a heartless cruel God bent on punishing the earthlings you've created. You can only be one or the other. So make up your mind, God, and show me your compassionate side!" At that moment I felt as though I was lost and didn't know where I was going.

I will always remember that day when I stood up to God.

I'm not one of those religious fanatics, who pray all day long with a rosary in their hands. Yet, on that day humbled by shame, I knelt on the prie-dieu, put my hands together and recited the Lord's Prayer at the top of my lungs—so that God could hear me. I cannot convey to you with words the impact the prayer had on me. I had made peace with my Maker, and it felt good. But there was one more thing I wanted to tell God: "Please . . . grant that twice two be not four." It was one of Ivan Turgenev's prayers.

A few days before Thanksgiving, a storm battered San Stefano with snow after snow. But the fury of the storm didn't prevent Mr. Cummings from arriving at Mon Plaisir. Always a man of exquisite taste, he walked in armed with a bulging briefcase and a leather valise (probably Hermes or Dunhill) for I cannot imagine him carrying anything less than elegant.

Mr. Cummings, a rather tall man with piercing hazel eyes and a longish nose, didn't mind being referred to jocularly as "The Shyster"; in fact he quite liked it. He and Uncle Hugh, both native San Franciscans, had met at Aux Assassins on Rue Jacob in Paris during the heyday of their boulevardier phase. Their friendship blossomed and continued all through Yale.

As far as I remember, they never missed a Yale-Harvard football game. And if Yale happened to be victorious, they partied with such éclat that they became legendary characters in the annals of New Haven.

After changing into more comfortable clothes, Mr. Cummings joined me in the library.

"Summer, let me begin by saying how enchanting is Mon Plaisir! Now I see why Hugh loved this place so much. My dear, I offer you my deepest sympathy. And I share your sorrow, for Hugh was a dear friend."

"Thank you. I appreciate your kind words and share your sentiment of love. Uncle Hugh was a very special human being," I said.

"As you know, I'm Hugh's legal council. I'm here for the sole purpose of carrying out his wishes," Mr. Cummings said, spreading a large dossier on Uncle Hugh's fine-grained Cuban mahogany desk with bronze fittings.

"Mr. Cummings, with due respect, let me tell you that Uncle Hugh's wealth is not the main issue here. I want to know, how did Uncle Hugh die? He went from a

142

perfectly healthy man to a dead man in a matter of weeks. Do I make myself clear?"

"Perfectly clear, my dear. Hugh's death was a simple mistake. There was no foul play involved. You've got to believe that."

"Please don't tell me what to believe, or what not to believe. I have my own thoughts on that matter. At gut level, I'm almost sure Daddy must have had something to do with it. But I can't prove it, yet."

"I'm absolutely honest when I tell you that there was no heart attack, no stroke, no bullet hole. And murder is out of the question. For God's sake! Why would anyone want to kill Hugh? He was loved by everyone. He didn't have an enemy in the world. His death was accidental, pure and simple."

"There is still a possibility that someone wanted him out of the way. But who and why? That's what I want to know."

"Of course, anything is possible. But . . . murder isn't one of them. What would be the motive?"

"I have this gut feeling that says Uncle Hugh fell into a carefully woven trap in one of Daddy's networks of lies."

"My dear, I'm satisfied with the coroner's report—death by asphyxiation. I spent hours exploring the effects of nitrogen gas exposure. All my findings led me to the same conclusion. Nonetheless, just to satisfy my curiousity in me, I questioned every one who might have seen or heard something that was out of the ordinary. According to one seasoned worker, it is possible Hugh was trying to retrieve the broken part of the locking mechanism of a tank hatch door, when he was overtaken by the fumes within and passed out. But, we can't be sure . . . for at that time Hugh was alone in the wine cellar."

"I can hardly believe that Uncle Hugh, a dyed-in-the-wool viticulturist with a master's degree in enology, would be careless enough to do such a foolish thing. Do you suppose this might be a simple case of suicide? If that's the case, I want to know why he chose Red Poppy to do himself in."

"Summer, my dear, perhaps your sense of loss is getting in the way of reason. I believe we have hashed this subject long enough, so let us return to the main reason why I am here. As I wrote, Hugh bequeathed his entire estate to you. The scope of the wealth is enormous."

"The wealth of money doesn't excite me."

"Well, anyway, Hugh's will makes you one of the richest ladies in San Francisco. The will gives you the house in San Francisco, Mon Plaisir in San Stefano, the charming maison on Avenue Foch in Paris, and his half of the Red Poppy in Sonoma County; as well as a huge stock trust."

"That is astounding, yet as meaningless to me as a fur coat in summer," I said hoarsely as though afflicted with laringitis.

"Hmmmm. Well . . . there is one more thing. Hugh's bequest infuriated your father. The truth is, he could not bear the thought of a woman making wine, especially you, his wayward daughter who had turned her back on the family. It's a bit of a macho thing. It's too soon to tell what your father intends to do. But if I were you, I would don a suit of armor and prepare myself for the battle ahead."

"Yes, indeed, Daddy is terribly clever, but his machinations will have little impact on me."

"Look—I'm not here to judge anyone. I'm only doing a job I've been hired for."

"Okay, Counselor; you've made your point."

"As soon as I return to San Francisco, I will proceed

with the probate. Where would you like me to send the papers?"

"I prefer San Stefano."

"As you wish."

"Thank you."

That very evening Mr. Cummings found me in the salon nursing a glass of cognac. He walked with a proud carriage, head held high, a pipe clamped in his mouth.

"Summer, you look divine. I must say that your new shorter bob is chic, and your gown is really very easy on the eyes. Now all you need is an Isotta-Fraschini cabriolet. And with your newly inherited wealth you can easily afford several exotic conveyances."

Mr. Cummings then said ruefully, "This may come as a surprise to you, but there was a time when I was not at all stodgy, but a devotee of fashion."

"I'm rather surprised."

"That's not all. My mother spent her money with great panache, and at her death, I inherited her exceptional serpent bracelet, made by the jeweler Georges Fouquet. Now I'm a devoted fan of the goldsmith's art," Mr. Cummings said and smiled quizzically. "However— returning back to you, I noticed that there is a certain curious exuberance in your eyes. I believe you're sneering at the world. What is it?" he inquired.

"You're very observant. As a matter of fact, I am hatching a plan that to get myself out of Daddy's clutches."

"I bet you were seeing yourself at the Red Poppy . . . making wines to rival those of France."

"Counselor, you are dead wrong."

"Well, whatever it was, it must be funny."

"Yes, it is. However, I will not elaborate, except to say

that I have recently visited an oracle, who told me I was a part of the Red Poppy's destiny. That I would be famous not for my wines, but for the stories I write. Of course, it depends on how you define famous."

"Summer, what makes you so certain?" Mr. Cummings asked gently.

"According to Webster's dictionary, famous is something known and talked about. In short, excellent. Now wouldn't it be swell if famous came with a set of instructions?"

"If only that were possible," Mr. Cummings said, standing to bid me farewell. "Well, my dear, the company was very good and so was the dinner. However, as you know, I have an early flight to catch. Thank you for your kind hospitality. *Bonne nuit, cher coquelicot.*"

The sound of the word "Coquelicot" took me straight back to Uncle Hugh. How dared Mr. Cummings to call me that? He must have known that corn Poppy was Uncle Hugh's secret name for me.

I was furious. How could Uncle Hugh betray me this way? I glanced at his portrait hanging above the fireplace. His eyes were serene with a touch of mystery. And suddenly I realized that there was something wrong with his mouth that I never noticed before. His lips were curled up in a mocking way, as though to puzzle a curious onlooker.

As I made myself look back at the picture, I wondered what had been Uncle Hugh's thoughts at the precise moment when the artist, all but forgotten today, put the last brush stroke on his mouth.

16

I broke through the doors of sunset
Ran before the hooves of sunrise.
                    —Francis Thompson

The blue-gray of the twilight changed to black; the sky was deep lustrous jet—more stunning, more incredible than anything your liveliest imagination can call to view. An extraordinary, unreal night.

I watched this all unfold from my bedroom, just a hop, skip and jump from the sea. Ah, to be a bird and travel to the moon on the wings of the wind, I whispered to myself as I tunneled into the uncluttered space of my bed.

Sometime during the night, when the moon was high up in the sky, I saw a shadowy apparition in the folds of the sheer curtains. A flicker of fear three degrees below panic crossed my face. I stood motionless as though carved from one solid rock. Curiously enough, I continued to view it along a spectrum that ranged from uneasiness to hysteria.

Now at loose ends with no comfort but the pines sighing in the breeze, I covered my head with the blanket and lay there creating fantasies about the ghost I had seen— yet at the same time praying that when I exhaled the ghost would be gone. No one who hasn't been visited by a specter can form any idea of the scary nature of such an apparition.

The next morning after that long night, it seemed that the ghost must have left the folded paper lying on my desk. Because I knew no living person had been in my room since yesterday, except for the phantom—and he was dead as a doorknob. By the time I recovered from the shock of that apparition I was almost crippled with anxiety and wonder. A basic part of me believed that the paper contained a poem written by Uncle Hugh. When I opened the paper I burst out crying as I had not done since Uncle Hugh's death.

> *Je t'aime, je t'adore*
> *Que veux tu de plus encore*
> *C'est mon coeur qui te le dit*
> *Et ma main qui te l'ecrit.*

Uncle Hugh (or rather, his ghost), had left a calling card.

Meanwhile, came the news that changed fantasy to reality: my first novel, *The Oratory of the Legends*, was going to be published. Finally I no longer was a nobody in literary circles! It was one of those crazy moments when you cry and laugh simultaneously like a demented soul. I believe this is the natural reaction of almost all writers, that flame of truth when they discover that someone besides themselves believes they have talent, after all.

In the spring of that same year there was a big shift in the British Secret Service. Unknown to me, but equally important, was the fact that I had been chosen to transport documents stolen from the German Embassy, located in the upper reaches of Pera. I was to work with Zulu, for Zulu himself had asked for me. I felt privileged, to say the least. It is not every day one is chosen to work with a famous espionage artist like Zulu.

The plan was to find out why the Nazi bureaucrat, Joachim von Ribbentrop, was en route to Constantinople for a month-long series of secret meetings with the Turks. Was he coming to secure the aid of an unnamed third party, possibly Russia? The Allies wanted us to provide them with the minutes of those meetings before the news leaked out and became a hot topic throughout the world.

For our meeting place, Zulu had chosen a small cottage, the sort of location where you might expect to see termite-eaten boards infested with cockroaches. According to local gossip, the shack which everyone discussed in hushed tones, once had belonged to a young sorceress, who ate raw meat, drank mule blood and bedded down with animals dressed in beautiful lynx skins.

Perhaps more than the sorceress herself, it was the cabin's location that terrified most people. Because it was nestled in a dark and shadowy cypress grove in the shoddy end of town, where at night prostitution flourished among the silent graves.

As a good luck charm before my departure to the shack that day, I wore my large blue eye hanging from a chain. I owe my life to that blue eye! But wait. I'm getting ahead of myself.

When I arrived at the shack, I discovered that the small daffodil patch had been trampled upon. The door was slightly open, which indicated that there had been a previous caller. I don't believe there ever was a time when I was more suspicious. My gut feeling told me to reach for my gun before I kicked open the door. A minute later, I was in another world, facing a man as stunned as I was, pointing his own gun at me. For a split second, I saw myself in the nightmare I had had in 1924. And I recognized the face. Nobody knows what happens in human beings when they are in the grip of fear. We cannot explain why bees sometimes kill their own queen, but we know that they do. I fired my gun, and down went the man in a confused heap. I squeezed the trigger and fired again and again. The man's shattered skull scattered in many directions. Who was he? His death barely dented my conviction that my action was not in vain.

As it turned out, I suffered only minor injuries because both bullets fired at me were apparently deflected by the big blue eye on my chest. I was very fortunate, wasn't I?

Meanwhile, Zulu arrived looking trim and debonair, his face as impersonal as a death mask. After he saw what happened, he uttered a few words in a sympathetic composure. "You see how things can go wrong," he said and dragged the man's body outside and covered it with leaves. In those days, in Constantinople, it wasn't uncommon for people to disappear, never to be seen again—especially if you were a spy. Once apprehended, no country (including your own) wanted to know you. That's the time when you reflect upon who is really the enemy.

Great relief came over me, like the last clap of thunder, when Zulu offered me a drink from a silver flask. We each lit a cigarette and watched the smoke rings dissipating among the ceiling beams. It was fun to watch Zulu smoke, for he did it so elegantly—each puff long and seductive. Suddenly, as though ready to switch gears, Zulu handed me an envelope, sealed with red wax.

"You know what to do, don't you?"

"Of course."

"Okay. Now it's up to you to deliver as instructed."

"Yes, I know."

Evidently, seeing traces of fear in my eyes, Zulu added, "Relax. Nothing terrible is going to happen to you—like in Germany when the Nazis beheaded two women for revealing military secrets to the enemy." That said, he tipped his cap and said, "Maybe when this war is over we can have a quiet dinner by candlelight."

"Perhaps . . . someday when we begin to dream better dreams."

As if spying wasn't excitement enough, now I suddenly had New York to deal with. But New York was another pair of gloves. It didn't take me long to pack two suitcases with my finest Turkish-crafted clothes. Probably, I was taking more than necessary; but spring in New York can, sometimes, be as capricious as a menopausal woman.

The overall plan was pleasant enough. I was to spend a few days in New York, long enough to negotiate a lucrative contract for my second book: *The Grand Metaphor*. It was (I hoped) an interesting book that defined the cutting edge of living in Constantinople in an era when God's Vice-Regents on earth and Crown of Veiled Heads ruled the city. Then I was to proceed with a cross-country promotional tour that would blitzkrieg through all major cities in the United States. The best part: a long stopover in San Francisco.

Oftentimes, as it happens with certain books, *The Oratory of the Legends* caught on big. Success . . . what is this thing called success? Let me paraphrase Fanny Burney. "He owed his success to the art of uniting suppleness to others with confidence in himself."

In the case of *The Oratory of the Legends,* it was quite obvious that my book had touched a chord in the heart of every legend aficionado with a large capacity for fantasy as well as reality.

In every bookstore, be it a small cubicle with its own idiosyncratic feel, or a large glitzy establishment with lots of fluff, the queues of potential readers, waiting to buy the book, were beyond imagination. I never dreamt a book could create such a brouhaha. Even by the publisher's standard, this overwhelming response was a tremendous rush, narcissistic enough to pump any new author's ego.

Finally, after days of train travel through cities with bright lights, I arrived at San Francisco on a perfect day, the air fragrant with class and quiet dignity. As soon as I was settled in my room at the St. Francis Hotel on Powell Street, I flung open my windows to drink in my beloved city, now locked between fog and sun. I was euphoric, yet I felt tired. I bathed in warm scented soap bubbles and crawled between impossibly soft sheets that smelled of lavender.

I remember the beauty of the following morning. The sky was as blue as a sapphire with a hint of fog. How enchanting was the sea, shimmering in the sunlight! More than anything else, I wanted to take a breather from my busy schedule, to wander through familiar streets, and to travel back to the happy scenes of my childhood. Instead, I showered and put on a yellow Chanel suit and a creamy-colored pearl necklace to light up my face. Today I was lunching with my old school chums at the Villa Taverna, and I wanted to make a splash in a stylish way.

I arrived at the Villa Taverna in the best of spirits, feeling as beautiful as San Francisco. Or at least I thought so. Yet when I saw my friends at the intimate restaurant, I felt like an old mother hen in a coop, herding a bunch of chicks with slow-ticking biological clocks. You see, my experiences had matured me way beyond my years. I was bright-eyed, but without the melancholy of youth that always gets in the way.

"Darlings . . . it's a stroke of good luck that brought us together again. It's simply grand to see you all," I blurted out, and kissed each one of them. They were a happy bunch of soignée women with glorious faces, perfectly content in their own world of hairdressers, dressmakers and milliners who worked tirelessly to make them look as though untouched by time.

"Gee! Summer, darling, you look ravishingly yummy," Barbara said and kissed me with her more than generous lips.

"Girls . . . girls . . . wow! It's like old times, isn't it? You all look marvelously young. What are your secrets?" I asked with a touch of envy, but without malice.

"Our secret is Royal Jelly. We eat it. We smear it," Barbara answered, playing with the precious stones around her neck. "And what about you, honey? What secret potions have you been using?" Barbara continued.

"Me? Nothing, really. I have no beauty secrets to speak of."

"Hogwash! Turkish women are famous for their beauty. Surely they must have a potion or two that you can tell us about?"

"Come on, Summer, tell us! We are your friends."

"Okay, I'll come clean. It's a combination of rice flour, almond oil, honey and rose water. Blend them together and pat it all over the body. That's my secret. Are you happy now?"

"Come on, Summer, you can be more candid than that."

"That's the honest truth. Almond oil will do it every time."

I had met Barbara during my freshman year at Yale. After graduating she married Archie Davenport, a rich, brainy man from San Francisco, who was an excellent equestrian with a stable of handsome thoroughbreds. I admired him only for his horses.

"Summer, darling, you are so damn thin! Don't they eat in the Ottoman City?" Sarah asked, studying her own reflection in the mirror.

"Honestly, I eat like a pig, I honestly do. Blame stress for my condition in the era known as hell."

"Despite all that you went through, you look smashing from head to toe, and from front to rear," Sarah said. She was as chubby as she was when we were teenagers.

"Hmm . . . by the way, your book, *The Oratory of the Legends,* is flying off the shelves. We always knew you were destined for true greatness," Jenny, my closest friend since first grade, said.

"*Tout* San Francisco literally cried when Hugh died. *Quelle tragédie*! It was all too sad," she continued, embracing me tenderly like she used to when I failed to pass a test. Jenny was the soul of kindness.

"My deepest sympathy, darling," Sarah cooed softly.

"Longfellow said it best when he penned the following verses," Jenny added, reciting the poem:

> There is a Reaper whose name is Death,
> And with his sickle keen,
> He reaps the bearded grain at a breath,
> And the flowers that grew between.

"This poem leaves me cold every time I recite it," Jenny added with a deep sigh.

"So why do you keep reciting it?" Barbara asked, seeing tears in Jenny's eyes.

"Oh! I don't know why. I just do it."

"Summer, we're all deeply sympathetic and wish there was something that we can do to alleviate your pain," Jenny said. "What are your plans for the future?"

That question threw me off track. Yes, what was I going to do now that Uncle Hugh was gone forever?

"Now . . . let me see. Tomorrow I'll be at the Orpheum bookstore for a Meet-the-Author party, which means more books to sell. Then I'm high-tailing out of San Francisco. I want to spend a few days at the Red Poppy before returning to Constantinople."

"What about Clouds? And your *chère maman*?" Sarah asked with a sugary sweet voice.

"Of course I would like to see them both. But these days I'm an unwelcome visitor. The whole point is, Mother refuses to give me an access key to Clouds."

"It seems so utterly cruel. To be honest, I never liked your mother. It's just that she always has seemed so—into herself."

"Well . . . Mother . . . was never a forgiving soul."

"But, there was one thing about your mother that stuck with me; her power to stop a charging hippo with her bare hands," Sarah added with a blush that could be seen through her rouge.

"Do you remember our long talks at Clouds, ensconced in twin beds, mirroring life in the grown-up world? I can still hear our laughter as we fantasized about the princes or the foxhunters who would whisk us to a farm in the heart of the hunt country where we could have hundreds of horses," Jenny rhapsodized, now eyeing a career in equestrian journalism.

"You bet I do. I never stopped wondering about those dreamers, who longed for the excitement of the marriage bed, yet craving secretly for the freedom to be themselves on their own terms," I said, recalling those moments of sheer rapture when we laughed even at a creepy cockroach crawling up mother's favorite bronze armoire.

"Summer, darling, put your wondering to rest. Except for you, most of those dreamers are still in midstream, still locked up in their own private jails," Jenny answered, twirling the gold band on her finger that she regarded as a symbol of lost freedom.

"Summer, darling, how serious are you about returning to Constantinople?" Sarah asked.

"I'm afraid I'm terribly serious. I love it there; Mon Plaisir is made up of lovely memories. I couldn't bear to live anywhere else. My destiny brought me there, and there I will die."

"My God, Summer, haven't you pushed that destiny thing a bit too far? However, I've got a wonderful idea, and I'd love to share it with you all, if you promise not to call me Brain Dead, like you used to do when I used to tell you about my dreams of becoming a prima ballerina," Sarah said, gazing sorrowfully at her fat ankles.

"Okay, you've got a deal. No name calling. But, what sort of idea is brewing now in that pretty head of yours?" Jenny asked, evidently remembering her dreams of becoming another Anna Pavlova.

"I'm dead serious. How about a party *entre nous* at the Red Poppy—to celebrate Trish's divorce?" Sarah asked.

"Divorce? What divorce? Please tell me more."

"Gee, Summer, don't get so huffed up. It's only a divorce, but with a murky side."

"Darlings, though I love the idea of a party *chez moi*, for reasons beyond my control—like my book tour—I will have to say no," I replied, in all sincerity. "I hope you're not too disappointed."

"Sarah, dear, I'm afraid this was another of your brain-dead ideas. But because we love you, we'll forgive you," Jenny said with a smirk.

"That said, let's return to the nitty-gritty of Trish's divorce. What happened? Who was the villain?" I asked, recalling that we were so envious of Trish at the time when she married Belton Phillips. Damn! "What fools we were to be taken in by his charms."

"Please, Summer; Trish was the fool, not us. Let's get the record straight, if you please," Jenny said with malice in her eyes.

"When Belton walked out on Trish, she was devastated. She was rushed to the hospital with serious wounds. Her maid, Annie, found her curled up in a pool of blood with her wrists slashed."

"Wow! Poor Trish. Is she okay?"

"She is not really okay, not okay enough to carry on with her life, but at the moment, she is engaged to be married to Dirk Donaldson. Do you remember him?"

"I don't believe I've ever met him. I'm curious. Was there a *femme fatale* who led Belton astray?" I asked, feeling that this juicy tale of love gone sour was ripe for plucking.

"It was Yolanda Pascali. The Italian *Charge d'Affaires'* exquisite daughter, a rare beauty with velvety black eyes, but mean. Yolanda moved into Belton's heart with all the slickness and slime of a snake," Barbara explained. "What really made me mad is that Belton thought he was so gorgeous that all women were there to worship him. In fact, I was one of the fallen women, for he was such a handsome dude."

"Girls, girls . . . I believe we have trashed Belton long enough. I hate to have to say good-bye, but I really must dash off. I'm having an early dinner *a deux* at Jack's."

"Hmm . . . it sounds naughty. Anyone we know?" Jenny asked, as inquisitive as ever.

"Relax. It's only Peter Wheatley."

"Mister World himself?"

"The very same."

"What's the attraction? Do you still find him irresistible, or what?"

"Goodness, no. This is just a friendly dinner to pick his brain—at least what's left of it. Peter is a third generation winemaker, who never imagined becoming anything else. As for me, I don't know if I have what it takes to make good wines. I need help to guide me through the winemaking maze."

"Your sudden interest in wine is quite understandable. Whatever you decide to do, we're behind you one hundred percent," Jenny said with genuine glee. "We promise to drink nothing but Red Poppy Pinot Noirs."

"Thanks for the support! Good-bye, darlings. Kiss, kiss. Please let's meet again next year. Same time, same place."

"What a wonderful idea. I love it," Jenny exclaimed.

"Don't forget the Royal Jelly. It will do you good," Sarah said. "And keep writing. Go with your passion," she yelled as I rushed out of the door.

Blessed with cotton candy clouds, San Francisco gave me back the San Francisco of my youth when going to Red Poppy was the highlight of summer. Oh God! How I longed to sprout my own wings and fly to the Red Poppy before the arrows were aimed at me as Daddy's target. Despite my desire to see Red Poppy, I had to put that wish on the back burner, at least for another day. Because on the following morning I was due to appear at the Orpheum Bookstore on Geary Street, to add my own brand of showmanship dazzle to the bookstore, itself a one-of-a-kind retailer with imagination.

By noon, the sun was a golden ball and the bay

gleamed like a big blue lagoon with just enough ripples to give it life. After weeks of shaking hands and autographing hundreds of books, I was anxious to high-tail it to Sonoma.

With my convertible's top down, I sailed across the valley, grapevines passing by in a blur. From a certain vantage point, I could almost make out a smaller me running across the fields, dressed in a white pinafore, chasing butterflies with my dog Jinga. This was a particularly joyous sense of *deja vu* after such a long time.

One image from the past that has not changed is Grandee, an old chestnut tree that has flowered every year since it was planted by Grandpapa, to celebrate the birth of his second son, Mizen, who died at the age of sixteen from consumption.

I parked my car under the magnificent shade of dear old Grandee. I cranked down the window and let my senses drink, smell, feel all that was Red Poppy. Suddenly, out of nowhere I heard voices—first as a murmur, then more clearly. Somewhere in the fig tree grove men were talking. One said to the other, "Guess what? I saw Mr. Grant's daughter drive in. You know the one they call the Black Sheep?" And another voice, crackling with irony, replied, "I cannot wait to see the old man's expression when they meet. Without a doubt the shit is going to hit the fan with a fury."

A short time later, I saw a man walking down the steps from the winery. I wondered who he was? He looked very familiar. I pulled down my hat over my face and hid behind the convertible door. Slowly, first with one eye, later with both eyes I peeked through the vent window near the dashboard. I saw that the man had changed direction. He was walking nonchalantly toward the fig grove beyond the grain elevator.

As I thought about the bygone age, I remembered the small door located at the far end of the tree-lined lane leading to the winery. It opened into a dark vestibule reeking of old wood. As children we used it as a hiding place. The carved wooden door was still there, and so were the two stone lions on each side of the door. I stood in the doorway holding my heart with one hand, and with the other a handkerchief to dry the tears running down my cheeks. This was an emotional coming home I hadn't banked on. I literally crawled into the room we always called Grandpapa's Doughnut, for it was a perfectly round room with a circular vaulted ceiling.

I have a memory of myself standing in the Doughnut, waiting to see which way the ball would drop. I heard approaching footsteps. Then a few minutes later I saw Daddy standing beneath the dome and blowing his nose. This was followed by a noisy cough—something he did when he was under stress. In a dramatic moment my eyes floated weightlessly toward Daddy's eyes, and they met in the most strange way. Neither one of us spoke. We were as motionless as two wax figures at Madame Toussaud's. My! How Daddy had aged. Despite the passing years, he had retained his handsome looks—so like Uncle Hugh's. It came as something of a surprise when he said, "Summer . . . really it's difficult to imagine that you are actually here at the Red Poppy."

"It is, isn't it? Well—hello, Daddy. How are you?"

"Oh! I'm hobbling along the best I can. And you?"

"Fine, just fine, thank you."

"I'm delighted to see you're looking so well," Daddy said and leaned forward as though wanting to kiss me. I stepped back. I felt sick and uncertain.

"Hmmmm . . . and how is Mother?"

"Mother is fine. Nowadays she is busy chasing aphids

instead of oracles. She has taken an active interest in roses, if you can imagine that."

"Hey, stranger things have happened before, when you stop to consider that Mother always marches to the tune of her own drummer."

"Summer...as you can see I've aged. Only God knows when I will say my final good-bye. Hence, when that time comes, I want to go knowing that you've forgiven me. Can you ever forgive me?"

"Daddy, sure I can forgive you, but I can never, never forget the pain, and humiliation that you caused Uncle Hugh and me. Poor, dear Uncle Hugh, how he suffered silently. Yet, despite your attacks, he never ceased to love you. I never understood the strength of the bond between you two," I said, choking on the energy of my own voice.

"By the way, these roses are for you. Congratulations! Local girl makes good. Here, let me give you a kiss."

"Roses...for me? How aristocratic of you. Thank you for the roses, but you can skip the kiss. I'm not quite ready for such a show of affection."

"Well—I'll overlook it this time. I'm very proud of you. Your book is a major achievement."

"I owe my success to Uncle Hugh. He alone was with me every inch of the way. He was that sort of a man."

"How generous of you to say so."

"Why not? It's the truth."

Daddy sighed, and paused long enough to light a cigarette and pour himself a drink.

"Dear Summer, because of what I've done, I'm doomed to live with the serpents of remorse forever, as penned by Pushkin."

"Speaking of serpents and other unsavory characters, brings to mind the question of Uncle Hugh's death. What really happened here at the Red Poppy, to push a perfectly healthy man over the edge?"

"A tragic accident...that's what occurred here. If you wish, I will show you the coroner's report. Perhaps then you can judge for yourself. It's best that you accept the coroner's account. Because there are no other explanations," Daddy said and took a big sip of his drink.

For a few minutes we sat in heavy silence.

"Summer, did I make myself clear?"

"I'm sorry to say, no—not clear enough for me. The mystery of Uncle Hugh's death is a nagging toothache that refuses to go away. It haunts me day and night and wherever I go."

"For God's sake! Why won't you accept the truth—like the rest of us?"

"Because I'm not the rest of you. You know that I know you are lying. Call it a gut feeling, or call it whatever you like. I don't know how to say it without sounding disrespectful. My gut feeling is, there's an angel who is trying to connect me with the truth. I want to know what you two talked about. What was the state of Uncle Hugh's mind? What did he eat? Where did he go? Who came to see him? Did he receive any mail? You get the picture, I hope."

"Seeking to learn the truth, as you put it, is going to do nothing but dredge up the past. What's the use of digging up old bones?"

"Daddy, you still don't get it, do you? In fact, it's you who is dodging the truth behind his death. As for me, I want to know everything about Uncle Hugh—everything from conception to death."

"Okay, fine, you've made your point. Truthfully, the verity of the matter isn't exactly what you would expect. It will be painful. It might even destroy you."

"Daddy, it seems so unfair for me not to know. I don't mean to pry into your life, but somehow, I feel you and

162

Hugh were bonded at the breast bone. And that's where lies the gospel truth."

Daddy stood up and walked to Uncle Hugh's portrait and back to me with a glacial look.

"Summer, first of all, let me say how much I loved Hugh. The rest is a fairy tale with strange twists and turns. According to my own legend, once there was a young man who fell in love with a beautiful maiden."

"Daddy, truly I don't need fairy tales. I need facts."

"Please, give me a chance to explain. To put it briefly, I had an affair. The young girl became pregnant and I made a big mistake."

"Well, then what? What is this all about?"

"I will continue with the story, as soon as I return from a short meeting, which is about to start. Meanwhile, walk around, read a book, or whatever you like to do. I promise I won't be long."

That evening, as I waited for Daddy to return, I felt like a hawk hanging on its outspread wings, waiting for the perfect moment to swoop and strike an unsuspecting prey.

There is something mysterious and melancholic about the dying sun, as it turns the woody vines into twisted golden rods. During this magical hour Daddy returned, his face as red as the glow of the sunset streaming through the wooden shutters. He seemed to be in high spirits, a crooked smile on his lips.

"Well, let's continue," Daddy said and sunk into a large leather chair.

"I thank you for keeping your promise."

"There are many things about me that you don't know. But, one thing for sure, I love this place."

"By the way, while you were away, I took a walk

through the winery. I should, of course, tell you what a wonderful idea it was to build the lobby with remilled redwood tanks. The scents alone give one the feeling of flirting with hundreds of grapes. It's simply magical."

"I'm glad you approve. However, the credit must go to architect Steven Broomly, who designed the room."

"What a clever way to use old tanks, and at the same time excite the nose!"

"And this is just the beginning of our growth. Now the experts tell us, the soil beneath the garrote of green oaks is ideal for growing world-class grapes. Grandpapa must be jumping with joy."

"Do you think our grapevines are robust enough to continue to produce fine grapes?"

"Beyond all question. I believe we have already, set the standard with our Pinot Noir, one of the best reds in California."

"You make Grandpapa proud."

"Now it will be your turn, Summer, to create new wines that would make the world proud."

"Oh, I don't know about that. Suddenly . . . I feel rather dubious about the future."

"Summer, I believe that you and I can work together to concoct wines capable of pleasing the best of noses and, at the same time, make them more interesting to the general public."

"If only I could believe you."

"It's not a question of whether you believe me or not. You see, I'm thoroughly convinced that we can join forces to reach heights in the global wine industry that only a few have achieved."

"Daddy . . . you have what some may call a case of super enthusiastic confidence."

"Summer, more important, perhaps, is that we both

love Red Poppy. Sometimes it takes a tragedy to make us realize all that we are blessed with. Don't you agree?"

"*Touché.*"

"Now let's go to the library where we can talk in complete privacy."

The scent of old leather mixed with the smell of wine nearly overwhelmed me. For a moment I felt as if I were jumping out of my skin. "Daddy, I'm feeling rather woozy. Let's open a window and let in the fresh air.

"Please excuse me for a moment, I believe I'm about to be sick," I said and ran out of the room, leaving Daddy rather awkwardly.

On the way to the bathroom, suddenly I heard the voice of my inner self speaking to me. "*The wine business is very exciting. But your goal was never to be a wine-maker. Your passion is writing. You know in your heart of hearts that you don't have the artistry of a good wine-maker. Face it, Summer, you were born to be a storyteller, not a half-assed viticulturist. So, my dear, forget it; let Daddy have the glory, if you can call it that.*"

I breathed a sigh of relief. I felt as though a heavy load had been lifted off my shoulders. Now there was nothing for me to do but tell Daddy that I wasn't interested in being part of the operation of the Red Poppy. One thing I felt sure of, if I were to stay here, surely I would soon wither and die—like a vine that is planted in the wrong field and at the wrong time.

Daddy was cheerful enough when I returned. Suddenly, he slipped his arm around my waist and said softly, "Summer, let's have a quick look around—so that you can see for yourself the tank in question."

"Do we have to do this?"

"It's best that you familiarize yourself with what I'm about to tell you."

Dim lights led us to the maze of cellars located in an adjacent stone building. As we entered, the air redolent of aging wine, I felt as if I were losing all sense of reality. I struggled with waves of nausea, like a woman going through the worst pains of childbirth. I tried to be a good sport and listen to Daddy while he talked about this wine and that wine, this method or that other method, oak barrels versus redwood—and so on and on . . . At that point Daddy had no idea what I had in store for him.

When we reached Cellar D on the north side, a sudden shiver flushed through my body. It was as if I were touched by a ghost too drunk to find its way back to infinity. And damned if I didn't get sick. Daddy suggested we leave now. But I insisted that I was okay and wanted to continue. The truth was, I wanted to go inside the Cellar D.

As we approached a slightly aged wine tank, displaying a small brass placard adorned with grape leaves, for no apparent reason I froze in my tracks, for I had the dreadful thought that perhaps this was the tank that had claimed Uncle Hugh's life. The horror of that moment squeezed my heart into a vise. I knew—just as an animal does when faced with danger—that this tank was something to fear.

"Daddy . . . there is something very eerie about Cellar D and this tank. Is this where Uncle Hugh died?" I asked, pointing at the large wine container.

"Yes, child. However, now it stays empty. The cellar rats are refusing to go near the tank, let alone age wine in it. These men are superstitious. They believe Hugh's spirit is still trapped inside, perhaps trying to get out," Daddy explained in a voice cracking with emotion.

"Daddy . . . I've seen enough for one day. It's cold in here! Let's get out before my tears freeze on my cheeks."

"Okay, let's go. I think we both can use some fresh air

and a couple of stiff drinks."

By the time we reached the Doughnut, the moon was halfway up the sky. Daddy poured two glasses of our own brilliant Zinfandel that had won the Grand Prix in Europe. Drinking that wine was like drinking pure sunshine. We toasted the ghosts of our kinsmen, making a point not to mention Uncle Hugh.

Daddy sensed my uneasiness.

"Summer... let's drink to Hugh. I tell you, child, he was a prince among men. Hugh was loved by all. You have no idea what his death did to me. It came close to destroying me, almost to the point of suicide. In fact, several times I held a gun to my mouth, but I never found the courage to pull the trigger. One day, shortly after Hugh's death, as I was going through his briefcase, I found an envelope, addressed to you. Now that you're here, you must take it," Daddy said and handed me a white parchment envelope.

The blood rushed to my head, as I struggled to control my heart, beating hard against my chest. I walked to the window and gazed at the vines sloping gently toward a stream. I became transfixed at the sight of a star so beautiful that it blocked off everything in the sky. Instantly, I knew that brilliant star was Uncle Hugh, wanting to be here. The glow stayed with me, as I read the poem—written on a paper stained with tears.

Stanbul
Adieu, Stanbul, adieu riant Bosphore!
Sombre cypres, vieux plantanes touffus!
Blanc minarets qu'un joyeux soleil dore
Je vais mourir, je ne vous verrai plus!

Forgive me, my sweet Coquelicot. It had to be this way. I

adore you, always will.
Your Buttercup

At last! The naked truth.

These were the thoughts of a man contemplating suicide. With this poem Uncle Hugh was letting me know, in
his own style, that he was intending to kill himself. The
worst feature of the note was that it lacked a more defi-
nite ending. I wondered about the secret message that
gave no explanation, other than to say good-bye.

However, a miracle was about to take place,
unknown to me.

The following morning, I found Daddy waiting for me
in the dining salon. It was a lovely room, its walls painted
with a powdered pigment in the traditional Andalusian
manner. As soon as breakfast was over, Daddy rose from
his chair, but stopped abruptly before the portrait of his
mother. He took a deep breath and crumpled to the floor.
Was he still alive? I was sure he had fainted. But a second
later, his shoulders shook and his hands curled inward
grotesquely as if he were maimed from birth.

"Daddy, what is it? Are you okay? Shall I call a doctor,
or an ambulance?"

He stared at me and said, "There is no need to call a
doctor. Just help me to sit up, please."

Little did I know then that this was a prelude to the
drama about to take shape.

"Summer . . . there is nothing like a great tragedy to
bring out the good and the bad in all of us. Forgive me, for
I talked with a forked tongue longer than I wish to
remember. Now I promise you what I'm about to tell you
is the gospel truth—so help me God."

"Whatever the truth might be, I'm ready to accept it."

"Summer, I've waited much too long to come clean.

The secret destroyed many lives in its path. Had I been honest right from the start, perhaps the truth might have saved Hugh."

"For God's sake, Daddy. What are you talking about?"

"There is much, too much to explain. However, it's best that I start from the very beginning, back to the time when I believed all of San Francisco was my backyard, and thought I was free to love as I pleased. In short; I had a mistress whose name was Laura."

"Well, that's a good start with romantic undertones. Go ahead with it."

"Well, my dear, love isn't all that's cracked up to be. Looking back, I believe I was quite happy with Laura. She was a remarkably talented girl with a God-given beauty. She delighted everyone—except Mother. Mother was dead set against me marrying a girl from the wrong side of the tracks. She simply couldn't accept her son wedded to the daughter of a lesser god. In other words; someone who wasn't in her precious Blue Book. You see, in those days, unions between the *haute monde* and the working class were taboo. Of course, Laura felt chastised," Daddy said, casting a cold look at his mother's portrait hanging next to his father's.

I thought to myself, *This story is beginning to get murky. And Daddy seems to be in the worst throes of human suffering.*

For a few minutes Daddy gazed at the silvery olive leaves trembling in the breeze. Then, after he had a chance to gather his thoughts, he continued. "Then came the terrible news. Laura was with child, my child. The news hit me like a ton of steel. At that point in time, Laura knew marriage was out of the question. I believe the shock of impending motherhood proved to be too much for her. She became obsessed with thoughts of suicide. In fact, one day I caught her trying to drink a bottle of iodine. As Pushkin wrote: Sufferance is sent to us from heaven; takes the place of happiness.

"Right there and then, we made a pact. She agreed to have the baby. And I promised to take the infant and raise it as one of my siblings. However, there was an additional condition. I was never to reveal to a single living soul the child's identity. The secret remained under wraps for years. But there came a day when I broke my silence. At one point in my life, I felt I ought to tell Hugh about the affair, while I had the chance. So when Hugh was here, I spilled the beans."

"But why now?"

"I only told Hugh because I didn't want to go on living a lie any longer, thus cleansing my conscience. And he had all the right to know about his roots before I stood at the Pearly Gates. Now the only reason I'm telling you about the circumstances of Hugh's birth, is because ... you see Hugh was not my brother, as you have been led to believe. *Hugh was my son,*" Daddy said.

I was dumbstruck. I felt every ounce of my being slowly dying. My lips trembled, my eyes become opaque. I couldn't move, let alone utter a single word. Thinking that perhaps I hadn't heard him correctly, I asked, "Daddy ... what did I hear you say? Did you just say that Hugh was your son, which makes him my brother?"

"Yes, Summer—you heard me right the first time. Hugh was my son by Laura."

I only vaguely remember the following minutes. However, I do recall seeing myself running through the vines with my eyes flooded with tears, asking God why this had to happen to me. The faster I ran, the louder I screamed.

My next memory of that day is finding Daddy

slumped in a chair, his inert arms dangling like the arms of a rag doll. For a second I stared at him without any emotion. To be honest, at that moment I wanted him dead. But, something deep down inside me made me go to him and comfort him with all the compassion that I could muster up. To my great amazement, with hatred came pity.

"Daddy, regardless of what you just told me, I have no regrets. I will never stop loving Hugh, whether as uncle or brother. You see, it doesn't make a bit of difference, really. Hugh will always be the crunch in my chocolate! Yet, I can't stop wondering about Laura. What ever happened to that poor woman?"

"Mind you . . . this is strictly confidential. After the birth of the baby, in a discreet hospital, the boy was immediately given to me. Laura never saw the baby, let alone nursed it. Soon after that, Laura entered a Carmelite convent in Chicago. I lost all contact with her. It was as though she never existed."

"Did you ever get over the affair?"

"Up to a point. There are still times when the guilt haunts me. But that is a small price to pay for all the happiness my son brought me. Hugh was everything a father would wish for."

"What about Grandma Grant? Did you ever tell her the truth?"

"No. I saw no reason to tell her. And if she knew, she never let on. She continued to observe the normal amenities of life, for the sake of the Grant name."

"And who cared for the baby?" I asked, for I felt a part of the unfolding drama.

"I engaged an English nanny, Miss Millicent Foster. I remember with great fun her pointy nose and her wide violet eyes. She catered to all the baby's needs in a nursery decorated with horses, wagons, trains and Indians with colorful head-dresses. Despite her inquiring nature, she never made any attempt to look further than the nursery. She loved Hugh as if he were her own son. Hugh was addictive."

"Hugh was a wonderful addiction. I can well understand Miss Foster's passion."

"As for the outside world, they thought I had adopted the only son of a dying friend. Period."

"Good show, Daddy."

"I'm glad you approve."

"That said, let us return to now and to Hugh's final days at the Red Poppy. If we set the time of his death as the time when you had your conversation with him regarding the circumstances of his birth, everything fits together perfectly. To my way of thinking, Hugh, noble to the end, couldn't accept the fact that he had deflowered his own sister. To his mind, this act of incest deserved nothing less than death. So it is with that chord of righteousness that he took his own life. We must respect him for that. As for you, Daddy . . . only God knows the final outcome."

"You know, Summer . . . in the final analysis, the true culprit is the life Hugh was born into, especially into a family like ours—dominated by aristocratic arrogance."

"Daddy . . . do you ever ask yourself what went wrong, really?"

"Only every minute of every hour."

17

God created man because He loves the stories.
                              —The Talmud

Shortly after Daddy's revelation, my stomach still in knots, I received an unexpected phone call from Paris. Salih, whom I had put on the back burner, was on the other end chattering like a bird about the delivery of his long anticipated Mercedes roadster. He wanted to go touring in France with me. Could I swing through Paris on the way back to Turkey? But wait. Here is the catch. About a week previously he had his coffee grounds read by a gypsy, who told him, "What I see is not pleasant to tell. Sometime soon an assassin will come looking for you. He will take a shot at you. Your wounds will be serious. You will not recover."

But however lucky I've been in this life to have friends, I never had one as sweet as Salih. Yes—you guessed it. The very next day I was on my way to Paris.

In this world where much is taken for granted, there are many hidden treasures that can be appreciated by simply coloring your imagination, which gives you a certain amount of control over your dreams.

During an era of innocence, my old-world upbringing allowed me to live in a world of my own making. As I traveled in my imaginary chariot over imaginary highways, often I saw myself in Paris as Sarah Bernhardt in *Theodora*, dressed in a cerulean-blue satin dress. And there were times when it was very easy for me to be at the Folies Bergère having a lively *tête-à-tête* with Toulouse Lautrec, while we watched the high-kicking can-can dancers raise the dust. Silly—but I also recall being Anne Boleyn on her way to be executed for alleged adultery. I can never forget the time when I sipped and supped with Simone de Beauvoir, Gertrude Stein, Scott and Zelda Fitzgerald and D.H. Lawrence at La Closerie des Lilas. Or perhaps it was at Aux Deux Magots.

On that brilliantly clear day in Paris, maybe it was my imagination coming to life. Or maybe it was the extra-ordinary time we lived in, or maybe it was Paris itself that caused me to grow a little sappy at the sight of the city's skyline. Whatever it was, I was in love, or at least I thought I was.

After making several dizzying turns through tree-shaded cobbled streets, intended for elegant carriages, the taxi slowed down and entered a mimosa scented lane, lovely enough to be visualized in one of my dreams. It was the sort of street where houses claimed more than ordi-nary affection from their owners, who were as *extraordi-naire* as the dwellings they called home.

The houses on Rue Manon, outside of the Chateau de Versailles, were famous for their crystal chandeliers. When darkness descended over the street, as by magic all the chandeliers came to life in the shape of glowing yellow flowers. However, the true spirit of Rue Manon was pas-sion—when lovers came to call on their mistresses, their arms laden with flowers. Each house had a story to tell. For example, Chateau Betyle, Salih's house, although it hardly seemed to correspond to the usual concept of a chateau, was once a French nobleman's love den. Just around the corner, Number Four, where stood the sculp-ture of The Three Graces, was the *casa* of a Spanish artist with an Italian poetess mistress. And Number Six, unlike the others, was a fairy tale of a house where you might expect to see either a satin-gowned or a calico-clad chatelaine, depending on her mood.

Salih's house was in a class all of its own. It was one of those places where your senses experience a visual shock at first glance. Everything in the house leaned a bit toward Ottoman splendor. Several ivory figures, depicting the four seasons, were suspended over a large period table. On another table was a large bronze figure of a hunter with two grizzly bears. Miniature horses and toy soldiers were arranged on a beautiful marble console. One entire wall was covered with a romantic landscape showing Salih standing on a tulip-shaped cloud. To be honest, I had never seen a garçonniere with so much whimsical class. This place was a far cry from my invented bachelor pads that were almost always overrun with pipes, ivory-handled revolvers, hunting guns, books and polo gear.

Looking back with nostalgic eyes, I think the most delightful memory of my Parisian *séjour* was the night when Salih took me to the Restaurant de Reverie on Rue Friolerie, off Rue de Rivoli. Although the restaurant has been altered over the years, I believe it still has its marvelous roof garden where the stars come out to play at night. Make no mistake, however—Reverie's expensiveness and exclusiveness were essential to its success. You see, Reverie catered mostly to the high-born with the scent of old money. It was for them that every night magic was created with bright flares that seemed to bond the roof garden with the sky.

Of course, everyone has their own idea about the restaurant. But the one thing about which they all agree is the music. To be more specific, "La Valse de la Lune," a spirited tune that had *tout Paris* waltzing in the 30s, as though seduced by the sound and its language of romance. As for me, my flirtation with the waltz was short of a physical intimacy, reminiscent of the dreams I had dreamed at the age of eighteen back in San Francisco.

As I recall, it was some time after midnight when we ducked in to La Porte Noire, an intimate boite for the city's cognoscenti. Within minutes we found ourselves sitting among colorful Bohemians, who were more interested in wine than in fashionistas in current style of dress.

That night, it seemed as if everything conspired to keep Salih and me happy. We held hands, laughed and drank; behavior that conjured up a host of possibilities and hopes. However, the merry mood was suddenly shattered when Salih asked me once again to run away with him and get married aboard the French luxury liner, the *Normandie*.

"Summer, chérie, I believe Allah brought us together for a special reason. It is His will that we should get married here in Paris. I see His blessing drifting down from the gardens of Heaven. Don't you get it? We were destined to meet. How else can you explain the bond between us? Please marry me before the assassin finds me first."

"Your offer is terribly nice. As you know, I suffered a great loss and I'm still mourning for a love gone forever. I hate to turn you down on such a splendid day, but this is an ill-timed proposition," I explained and burst into tears, for frankly, I felt unhappy (which can't be explained in a hundred words).

"Why are you afraid to marry me, really?"

"Well . . . mostly I'm afraid of the Armenian vendetta, which could make me a widow at forty-something. Also I

176

fear that someday when you're tired of me, you'll simply clap your hands thrice and say the formulaic: I divorce you, I divorce you, I divorce you—and just like that I'll be cast aside like yesterday's news."

"O Almighty God! Never would I let you go—even when you're old, feeble and ready to be buried in a forgotten grave. As for the Armenians, they have to catch me first; I have survived many attempts on my life. And each time I fooled the man with the scythe. But—that's not saying my future is secure, for it's not. Nothing in life is."

"Salih ... I believe this sudden urgency has come about because of one fortune-teller's prophecy. Please don't let a gypsy's words become your reality! Also, there are things about me that will shock you. My closet is full of bats who fed on blood for a long time. If they could talk, you might feel differently about me. Maybe even hate me."

"I can never hate you, Summer. I've loved you from the moment when I first laid eyes on you. Nothing will change that."

"I like to think that we love each other enough to wait for the right time. Then what a joy our life will be."

"I hope I'm around long enough to attend my own wedding," Salih replied with a faint smile.

Reader, don't think of me as an evil person for breaking the heart of a gentle man. You see, the truth is I was scared of the Armenians. Their preoccupation with the Turks had turned into an obsession. Killing a Turk was a part of every living Armenian's descent.

"Summer, it appears to me that neither of us have any choice in the matter. You have to return to Constantinople and I will continue to dodge the Armenian bullets here alone. So a swift marriage is the answer."

"I'm sorry that's not possible. Why not return to Constantinople yourself? Here there is the smell of death. Armenians have rooted themselves into the fertile French soil. They seem to be everywhere."

"Really, it doesn't matter where I go. They will find and kill me whether I'm in Paris, Constantinople or in a remote village in Africa. The handwriting is on the wall."

"Stop it! Stop it now, I say! This morbid conversation is beginning to give me goose bumps. Come on, lighten up. Let's drink to the future before the future becomes history."

We had barely raised our glasses to toast ourselves, when a bullet from somewhere within the establishment whizzed over Salih's head and into the glass he was holding, shattering it into many pieces. This had to be the bullet of the same Armenian assassin.

"Salih, you're in terrible danger! There is someone out there who wants to do away with you. Please fall to the floor and pretend that you're dead. Don't move, don't make a sound. Don't even breathe! Let the assassin believe that he won," I ordered as though instructed by Zulu.

Obviously, Salih wasn't destined to die just yet. Now the challenge was how we were to get out of La Porte Noire without being noticed. Perhaps the safest exit was through the back door that opened into an alley filled with drunken passersby. For us to stay on was to invite the fate that had befallen other Turks in Paris and elsewhere.

By all accounts the vendetta against the Turks was a just cause whose time had come. After all, the Turks' terrible atrocities committed against the Armenians were legendary—never to be forgotten. Bear in mind that thousands of women and children were made to march across the Syrian desert to Aleppo under impossible conditions. Their suffering, and the fact that only a few had survived to talk about their ordeal in the desert, was extraordinary enough to turn ordinary citizens into supporters of the on-going assassinations.

One of my favorite keepsakes is the memory of that long-ago night in Paris—when I blamed the adrenaline coursing through my body for the way I let down my guard. On second thought perhaps it was the breath of death disguised as the Armenian bullet. I will never know for sure, but for the sake of argument, let's say that it was in keeping with the Rue Manon's reputation.

Imagine, if you please, a secret garden in the heart of Paris devoid of humanity, but ringing with bird songs. You are young, in love and alone with a man who's decorating you with garlands of flowers. The sudden brush of the soft petals against your skin creates in you the erotic feelings known as passion and lust. After months of dreaming about such sweet moments, you are eager to relinquish your virtue for the sake of love.

As for me, the next thing I remember, besides the roses climbing from the sides of the house to the roof, is Salih and me rolling on the soft jasmine-scented grass. Kissing, caressing, cajoling our senses in grand style, exactly what one would wish in a dream. This was fantasy at its most recherché, and I saw no reason to return to reality.

"Summer, be honest. Don't you love me?"

"Of course I do. Why do you ask?"

"Because you're a bit of a puzzle. You let me make love to you, yet you refuse to marry me. Your modus operandi boggles the mind—at least, *my* mind."

"Salih, for God's sake, let us enjoy the moment and stop psychoanalyzing the process. You are gentle, sensitive and intelligent and I love you to distraction."

"I'm sorry, Summer. Sometimes I'm so unsure of your love."

"Here . . . let me kiss you again, for I owe you a great deal. And if all goes well, our wedding will take place sometime next year. Now that should chase away your fears."

Reader, I don't believe there is any further need to elaborate. It's best that I let you build castles to your own imagination. But let me say on my behalf that on that night in the garden of thousand senses I created a new legend.

As anyone who has been to Paris knows, one of the pleasures of the City of Lights is walking and composing fantasies in your head and forgetting who you are, where you came from and where you are going. Whether you pursue the heavenly scent of fresh bread in an alley lined with small shops straight out of a Utrillo painting, or eat in an old café served by a waiter whose shoes creak, the experience is a pilgrimage.

On that third day of my arrival, Paris sparkled under clear, azure skies. I felt the city's magic rubbing on me. I was eager to see everything at once: The Bibliothèque National, the monuments, the churches, the parks, the cafés where Hemingway, Fitzgerald, Colette, Beauvoir and Sartre sat for hours nursing their coffee or wine encompassed by the eternal heartbeat of Paris.

On the way to the Bohemian Quarter, Salih and I stopped at the Café Flore to munch on buttery crois-sants and millefeuilles with soft custard between the layers. Besides serving the best coffee in town, Café Flore was where many Parisians came to play out their fantasies and to reinvent themselves. According to local gossip, Flore is a sidewalk theatre where anything can happen—and usually does.

Perhaps it was fate, maybe it was mere coincidence that we stumbled across Josephine Baker at the café. Honestly I don't remember how all this came about. Suddenly, high-keyed voices, like notes in an unknown scale, were drowning Flore's gentle buzz. People from everywhere were yelling, "She is coming, she is coming! L'Étoile Noire is coming!" To all intents and purposes, Josephine Baker (also known as L'Étoile Noire des Folie Bergeres) was *une Americaine Negresse* who had earned her place in the sun. Her sheer presence left all who saw her mesmerized.

Perhaps I'm getting ahead of myself. But I think it's very important for me to mention that the front of the café was cluttered with umbrella-shaded tables, and people sitting reading papers under leafy trees, reflecting each other so closely that one had trouble seeing beyond their heads.

Salih and I were exchanging gossip over large cups of café-au-lait, when we saw two women and two men on bicycles glide by. They were followed by a most curious sound—like a wave crashing on rocks. I looked up and saw a statuesque black woman on the sidewalk surrounded by people of many colors and sizes. A sudden turn of a man's head out of her entourage made me nervous. There was something disturbing and frightening in the way he stared at Salih and me. He was a rather short, stocky man with an olive-colored complexion and hair to match. Soon anxiety gave way to joy, as I saw Miss Baker and her accompanying group go around to a large table placed in the shadows. It was about then that I realized I had lost sight of the man. In that split second when your senses are at war with each other, a bullet whistled over our heads and lodged itself in the wall behind us. People got up from their tables and rushed into the street, taking cover wherever they could. The habitués were confused and began to yell for help. Meanwhile, another bullet was fired from another direction. That bullet pierced Salih's eye. He gave a faint cry and collapsed onto the floor.

Now stunned beyond reason, I felt like a rag doll that had been bathed in bubbling lye. I must have fainted. When I regained consciousness, the first thing I saw was the face of a gendarme leaning over Salih's body. Then I took notice of a priest at Salih's side reciting a prayer. By then I knew that Salih was dead. I saw no need to ask God for another chance.

"Mademoiselle, you were very brave to shield your friend with your body. Because a moment later another shot rang out. But that bullet, too, lodged itself into the wall. However, it appears that the assassin's sole goal was to kill your friend, not to take additional lives. Because just as easily he could have killed you," the wide-chested priest said and put the rosary back into his pocket.

Meanwhile the French police had alerted the Turkish Consulate. They sent one of their own to take charge of Salih's body.

Now the first order of business was to get myself out of Paris. The prospect of spending the night in Salih's house, still echoing with the sound of his laughter, held little appeal. Yet I went to Betyle to spend one more night with memories. The deadly silence pressed on my eardrums, to the point of agony. To make matters worse, there were no early morning flights out of Paris. The best they could do was to put me on a flight leaving Paris at 3 P.M.

The next day I was at the airport at noon, prepared to leave Paris to the Parisians.

In an amazingly clever sweep, the French police arrested a young man, believed to be an Armenian, on his way to the Sorbonne. The man, also called The Spirit, readily agreed to cooperate. He gave the police the Mauser 32, the alleged gun used to kill Salih. After telling to the police that he was an Armenian, a student at the Sorbonne University, he seemed relieved that he had been taken in custody. When he was told he was under arrest for killing an unarmed man, he showed no sign of fear and in fact appeared unconcerned by the prospect of death. However, he requested that his body be returned to his village near Lake Van in Turkey. Then for a moment he grew uneasy and said with wry humor, "It is incredible to think that I was able to kill him with a single bullet, after all."

The alleged assassin, Mardiros Mardikian, was not your typical gun for hire. He was highly educated and articulate. Using his fingers to emphasize each point, he explained quite eloquently why he had fired the gun with intent to kill. In his sworn affidavit he said, "I am an engineer by training. I have plotted to kill a Turk for a long time. Of my own free will I armed myself with a gun and set out to avenge the death of my father and thousands of other Armenian men who were tortured and left to die with horseshoes nailed to their bare feet—by a so-called enlightened man—the then Turkish Governor, Djevet Bey, who was known throughout Asia as the Blacksmith."

At the trial, Mardiros Mardikian summed it up briefly, instead of launching an attack of words.

"The Turks declared war on the Armenians. There is bad blood between us. As long as there is a world, we will remain mortal enemies. You see, the death of one Turk gave voice to thousands of silent Armenian corpses, who could not stand up to speak for themselves. I am their voice. I am their spirit. I am their hope. I do not fear God's backlash. Only, I am sorry that I killed an innocent son for his father's sins. But he was a Turk and his father was Sultan Adbul Hamid. May God have mercy on my soul; I will die for what I believe was just."

By all accounts, true to his character, Mardiros Mardikian went calmly to his death. Little did he know that he was to become an instant national hero, as the rock that crushed the spirit of Djevet Bey in a blind force of fate.

18

Those who do not feel pain
Seldom think that it is felt.
—Samuel Johnson

No one knows whether or not the brilliant month of June hung its infant clouds over Paris intentionally, in a gesture of sympathy, on that day when Salih's remains were shipped to Istanbul. Perhaps it arranged things for Paris as if to impress the mourning Turks that Paris was not a city short of soul.

In the past, obsessed with thoughts of death at the hands of Armenians, Salih had shown an interest in the Mihrimah Jami mosque, built in 1562 by the Imperial Princess Mihrimah, who wanted to shine in her own right. Respectful of the culture into which he was born, Salih believed the mosque was the perfect resting place for the son of Osman and martyr of his time.

In a diary I kept during those trying days, I wrote about the Turks' frustration veering between indignation and revenge. The Turks felt that no son of God's Shadow on Earth deserved to die without knowing how many Armenian slugs were embedded in his skull. They announced angrily that no peace was possible between the combatants—not until flowers bloomed in hell.

Meanwhile, November arrived in Istanbul shrouded in black. The great Ataturk, the Father of all Turks, was dead at fifty-five. He took his last breath at five minutes past nine on November 10, 1938.

He lay in state for three days at the Dolmabahce Palace. On the fourth day Ataturk's ebony casket, draped with the Turkish flag, was carried down the wide staircase and into the street where it was placed on a gray gun carriage drawn by soldiers. An officer too young to remember the Turkish victories at Gallipoli walked behind the carriage with precise steps, eyes fixed on the casket. He carried a small velvet pillow displaying a single medal, that of the War of Independence. No greater honor was possible for the man who was largely responsible for changing the face of an entire nation.

As the procession wound slowly toward the Galata Bridge with the assistance of the police, all other traffic was halted. I can never forget the way Ataturk's devoted subjects cried out in grief and fell to the ground to kiss the coffin's shadow as it passed over well-trodden cobbles, there since the early days of Byzantium.

How many, one wonders, noticed the sudden eclipse of the sun at the height of this sorrow? But I saw it, because I was there standing among the river of mourners, estimated at ten thousand. They carried flags and portraits of their idol and all were trying to catch one last glimpse of Ataturk's coffin before it was placed on the waiting gun boat for its final journey.

Ataturk wished to be buried in his beloved village across the plains and mountains of Anatolia, near Ankara.

Despite my promise to visit the cemetery someday to place a blanket of red tulips on Ataturk's grave, I never did.

Only a few years later, the world was on a steep downward dive.

On December 7, 1941, Japan attacked Pearl Harbor, the U.S. Naval base in Oahu, Hawaii, destroying *U.S. Virginia* and *U.S. Tennessee*. This sudden attack created a gush of patriotism from San Francisco to New York. Immediately the U.S. interned 100,000 Japanese Americans.

In March 1944, Allies cut off arms to Turkey because of its reluctance to fight the Axis.

The Allies, under the command of General Eisenhower, landed in Normandy on June 6, 1944. Eisenhower addressed the people of Western Europe over the airwaves: "This landing is the opening phase of our campaign in Western Europe. Great battles lie ahead. I call upon all who love freedom to stand with us."

However, it was the *Enola Gay*, piloted by Colonel Paul W. Tibbets, Jr., and the atomic bomb's mushroom cloud of boiling dust and churning debris to spread terror far beyond Hiroshima and Nagasaki and end the war.

There were more surprises yet to come: American and British Armed Forces arrived in Istanbul. They were a new presence that changed the tempo of the ancient city.

Suddenly, all over Istanbul people were chewing Wrigley's gum instead of mastic, the favorite of Turkish women for centuries. Looking back on those bygone days, I remember the sudden love affair of the Turkish men with the American cigarettes—Marlboros, Camels, Chesterfields and Philip Morris.

Meanwhile, in Pera and in other sections of the city, houses of prostitution were doing brisk business, exploiting young women, some as young as sixteen, dressed in scanty clothes much too revealing at any age. Johnnies were the men of the hour and dollars and pounds were the currency of choice.

As for me, I tried desperately to console myself, as best as I could, for Istanbul's loss of serenity. Because the Constantinople I lived in yesterday is not the same as the Istanbul I live in today. Of course, no one will ever know what this means, except those of us who once resided there.

So we covered our eyes and ears to all the things that hindered understanding and accepted the new way of life in the city. In time we all learned to give no heed to the sound of Jeeps bouncing on cobblestones, echoing all over Istanbul. In the midst of the ongoing hubbub, dances were held at the USO and the Alliance Française, which led to many affairs in intimate boudoirs with silk drapes, and in not-so-intimate rooms with calico curtains where bedbugs scurried across sheets embroidered with flowers.

During that time a throng of babies born out of wedlock became facts of war. Heavily-rouged young girls sold their bodies for a few liras, a carton of cigarettes and some Hershey bars.

In the summer of 1946, when June had barely started, while the world was still trying to dig itself out from under the rubble, I reached a new milestone; I turned forty-two.

Then an amazing thing happened. By sheer chance I met an American Colonel from Maine. Not to keep you in suspense, reader, let me tell you how it came about.

From time to time, I found myself attending the USO dances in Pera. What I cannot explain is why I picked that particular night to saunter into the commissary, dressed in a ruby-red dress with a long sash. Come to think of it, perhaps I wanted to celebrate the publication of my second book, *The Grand Metaphor*, to critical acclaim. Or maybe it was to fulfill another of the Mouse

Oracle's prophecies: Happiness will come dressed in a uniform.

The memory of Mme. Kappa's words conjured up a new host of possibilities. And the possible candidate came in the shape of a tall man with broad shoulders and a smile to match. The person in question is like a photomontage. You really don't believe it, yet you know this person coming into focus is a composite of different parts that have blended together to create a human being.

What I remember about meeting the officer was his eyes, which were bright blue. As he came closer his gaze locked with mine.

I was very excited; panic seized me with both arms. I felt my matching beautiful ruby-red shoes freezing to the floor like cabbages in the winter. The officer smiled and offered me a glass of beer. I returned his smile and thanked him for the beer. A second later he simply said, "Hi," exposing a marvelous set of white teeth. "By the way, have we met?" he asked, quite nonchalantly.

"Have we?" I asked. "Because if we had, I'm sure I would remember you—unless I was blind or dozing in a chair with a blanket over my head."

"Gee! How lucky can a man get in one night? A beautiful woman with a sense of humor. This has to be a windfall from Heaven. Thank you, Lord."

"Ordinarily, I'm not so clever with one-liners. Though sometimes I can be witty when the situation calls for it."

I recall thinking he was a handsome devil but he probably was married with six kids and two dogs.

"Honestly, you look so familiar! I can swear I've seen you somewhere before. Yes, I'm absolutely sure of that."

"I doubt it. On the other hand, maybe we met in a previous life. We might have been related through marriage."

"Just maybe we met on Mars or Pluto."

"Hogwash."

"Listen, I'm serious. It would be a sad day in Heaven, if I were to forget a face as lovely as yours," the officer said with a wink.

"Anyway, for the sake of argument, let's just say that we had met. Okay . . . now what?"

"Wait a cotton-picking minute, it's all beginning to come back. I know where I saw you. It was in a school photograph. Did you attend Miss Porter's in Connecticut?"

"Matter of fact I did. Why do you ask?"

"This is so unreal, so weird, to say the least. My sister Alexandra, known as Foxy, attended Miss Porter's, too. Holy cow! Imagine meeting you here, of all places—Istanbul."

"Hey! Thank your lucky stars we didn't meet in the belly of a great white shark."

"Does it really matter where we met? The point is, we met. Let me introduce myself. I'm Percy Todd Spencer from the wonderful state of Maine. I graduated cum laude from Exeter Academy. I cut short my studies at Harvard to join the Army."

"I'm Summer Grant. And I'm a different pair of gloves. I was born during a thunderstorm in San Francisco, California. Also it's only fair that I should tell you, once upon a time, I was an adorable baby, who pooped in her diapers just like any other baby. But, with one exception. My poop went to a bathroom with gold-plated fixtures."

"Yours is a classic case of old money mixing with new poop! But what I want to know is what are you doing in Istanbul? Are you attached to the American Embassy, or are you working at the American Hospital?"

"Yes, you want to know why I am here? Let me count the ways, but it might take all night. So it's best that I tell you right away—I'm a writer who enjoys working among the old Byzantium ruins."

"I declare! What do you write about?"

"Legends, myths and other phenomena. In other words, I play with the pictures of my creative visualization."

"What a novel idea. I approve."

"I was fortunate enough to have a mother who loved legends, and she always insisted that I should read old tales, for they were more nourishing than contemporary literature."

"How about real stories of real people?"

"I stay clear of them. I'm into folksy tales. They are my passion. Now I believe I've talked long enough about myself, I don't want to bore you to tears! And what about you? What makes you tick?"

"Okay, you're in for a surprise. Once, I collected bears, all sorts of bears. I must have hundreds of them. But, my all time favorite bear is Joy. Joy and I go a long way." I did not ask him to elucidate further. I merely accepted his statement, knowing we were kindred spirits, through our bears.

"How would you like to go to a café" he asked, "where they don't play over and over, Diana Durbin, Harry James, Bing Crosby and Glenn Miller? I know of a funky old place near the tunnel where Loti used to go. Ditto Marlene Dietrich. It is an easy-to-miss hole-in-the-wall café that's worth seeking out for its perfect blini and bottles of the best local vodka."

"Sounds good to me. Let's go."

"Okay," Percy said and stood up to help me with my shawl.

191

God knows I've done many foolish things. But this flight of fancy was nothing short of crazy. Here I was on my way to a café in a remote part of town, with an American soldier I hardly knew. And this was a café known for its blood-chilling ideology of Russian Bolshevism. But, during those uncertain times, people often took chances on friendship.

On that night, Café Gubish was packed with all sorts of Russians, milling around the tables. Some were dressed in shirts embroidered with blue flowers, and others wore faded uniforms and caps. Among them a few uniformed "Pharaons"—the slang name for policemen used by the Russian revolutionaries.

A portentous man of sixty-something directed us toward a table placed in an antechamber, converted from a closet. Apparently, this space was reserved for the modernists, coming into their own. A loud burst of applause followed our order of blini, caviar and vodka. Never mind the excitement. What really mattered was the fact that we were immediately accepted into the fold—despite Percy's American Army uniform.

"Summer, did you know that the blini was created in the sun's image and eaten in the sun's honor? However, this café carries it a little further by adding saffron to the dough, to give it a more sun-like color. Tonight, I've ordered them in your honor. Because you are as bright as any sun in the universe!"

"Really . . . how swell of you. But I would have been just as happy with hamburgers and French fries."

"Hamburgers in Istanbul? This is not the American Heartland, you know."

"Percy, what puzzles me most, is how you found this café in the first place. I had heard through the grapevine that this shop attracts interesting revolutionaries, students and members of the Russian intelligentsia, and it is where the ideologies of the left are supported by the educated elite."

"I myself, a law student, enjoy listening to their fiery debates of the specified question. And, without a doubt, this café has the best blinis in town."

"Once, a long time ago, a Yalie told me that all Harvard boys were revolutionaries at heart."

"Well, depending on the cause, most Harvard boys are willing fighters."

"In my family, it's a tradition to attend Yale. But, because of you, I'm beginning to like Harvard boys. Regardless of my present fondness, keep in mind that no Grant boy goes through life without attending Yale. So, you see, when push comes to shove I'll always side with the Yalies. I hope you can deal with that."

"Don't worry. I understand. Because I feel the same way toward Harvard."

No matter how much we talked, it seemed as though we had just started. Percy had an unusual talent for evoking the past—its essence as well as the sights, sounds and smells. By the time the blinis had come and gone, we were ready to climb into each others' skin. We laughed and blew bubbles at each other. We held hands and giggled like two teenagers out on their first date. It went on and on until the wee hours of the morning.

By the time dawn had broken over the city with the entire spectrum of the red, Percy and I knew that we wanted to spend the rest of our lives together. We were each other's bonds. I saw possibilities offered to me on golden platters. Because my gut feeling told me that Percy was capable of blooming roses out of ashes.

"Summer, it's morning. Now that we've familiarized ourselves with each other's most sacred secrets, let's go a little further—like exploring our senses beyond our skins," Percy said boldly and I felt blood rush to my cheeks.

Something in my heart lurched. The possibility of us having sex so soon in the game had never entered my mind. I knew full well what exploring our senses meant, but I acted coy and asked, "What on earth do you mean?"

Percy held my hand and kissed it. "What I meant was . . . in a word: sex. Did I shock you?"

"Well, sort of. How times have changed. Now everything seems to develop legs to move faster and faster."

"Well, my dear, in the theatre of war there is no time for tomorrows, because tomorrow may never come. And it's not as though you have to climb over a wall!"

"Well . . . don't you think it's rather too soon for such personal contact?"

"Summer, it was to be expected. You're making far too much of this."

We laughed together about it.

On the way back to San Stefano, something very unexpected happened in the taxi. Just like stars that appear suddenly in the sky to take your breath away, in the blinking of an eye I found myself entwined with Percy's body. We stayed in that position for the longest time with locked lips and arms around each other in an abstract way. With each amorous caress I could feel the threads of my heart unraveling one by one. But I knew these erotic desires had to be squelched and quickly.

My heart jumped into my throat when the taxi suddenly came to an abrupt stop in front of La Porta, an old convent transformed into a charming hotel with circular columns to define the outdoor space and make it more intimate. I was stunned, yet secretly overjoyed.

Percy asked for a room overlooking the city. He had

barely signed the hotel register when in a sudden rush I was scooped up in his arms and he ran up the stairs with wide views of the Golden Horn. To any prying eyes there could have been no doubt as to why we were in such a hurry to reach our room on the second floor. Now liberated from curious and questioning glances and maids dashing in and out with baskets of fruits and flowers, we felt free to be ourselves and do as we pleased. Percy eased my dress down and sat me on the edge of the bed, still wearing my flesh-colored silk panties and bra. Then he took off his jacket and undid his belt. He folded his officer beige pants and set them next to his jacket. Suddenly, he leaped onto the bed and put my head on his shoulder. In a wild kissing frenzy we rolled to the floor. Everything flowed beautifully.

I slithered like a snake into his arms and closed my eyes. I found the warmth of his body as soothing as warm silk. Suddenly, I felt the room spinning around me and my heart beating fiercely. We were at the climax of sexual excitement with simultaneous orgasms. Even more extraordinary, this passionate scene was repeated over and over, until our emotions were totally spent.

I laughed inwardly thinking about my bargain with Aya Fotini. Perhaps the happiness I felt was her gift to me for keeping my end of the bargain?

We talked almost nonstop all the way to San Stefano. As we drove through the gates of Mon Plaisir panic seized power. I didn't want to say good-bye, for I knew my happiness now depended only on being with Percy. He walked me to the door and kissed me with such passion, I felt my lips melting into his. For a few delicious moments our lips were unable to break their magnetic pull.

Percy called me the very next day, and the day after, and the day following the last day. He gave me the impression that he needed me as much as I needed his energy in order to exist. Do you think I was silly to think that maybe we were Siamese twins sharing one heart?

The next few months were exciting. My diary is full of entries of our feelings, our love, what we did, where we went. It would be fruitless to deny that during this time nothing urged me on like Percy's love. This was the spring of our contentment. As the weeks continued, Percy expressed an impatience to get married. He saw no reason for a long engagement...

And in sports-obsessed America, Maury Rose was winning the thirty-first annual Indy 500; the Yankees won the World Series against the Brooklyn Dodgers; the French racer, Jean Robie was bicycling at the first Tour de France; and my own personal triumph, was the publication of my third book: *Hopes and Realities*. And best of all my impending marriage.

This much is certain, but the future events are shrouded in mystery.

...On December 8, 1947, the following wedding announcement appeared in the San Francisco Chronicle, the Voice of the West:

SUMMER GRANT, AUTHOR OF
THE *ORATORY OF THE LEGENDS*
MARRIES COLONEL PERCY T. SPENCER

Miss Summer Grant, a third generation San Franciscan, daughter of Mr. and Mrs. Jack Grant of San Francisco, California, was married on November 2, 1947, to Colonel Percy Todd Spencer, known as Master of the Hounds, the son of Mr. and Mrs. Whitney W. Spencer of Augusta, Maine.

Miss Grant was exquisite in her bias-cut gown by Balenciaga and wearing Cartier's diamond earrings. Her veil of point-appliqué lace, which had been worn by two other brides in her mother's family in France, was gathered into a tiara of tiny white roses and deep red rubies, a splendid touch to the gown's long train.

The ceremony took place in the Church of St. Mary in San Stefano, Turkey, and was followed by a reception in the gardens of Mon Plaisir, the bride's enchanting villa on the Marmara Sea.

For their wedding trip the couple traveled to Bursa, the historic first capital of the Ottoman Empire. They will make their home in San Stefano, Turkey.

Among my fond memories of the reception, there is one moment when I thought I felt the brush of an angel's wings against my face—and I will hold this feeling in my heart and soul forever and ever. It is possible within the framework of imagination that the angel was Uncle Hugh who had returned to his beloved Mon Plaisir to wink and smile and quote a small passage from Azel Munthe's book: "I am the immortal spirit of this place. Time has no meaning to me. Two thousand years ago I stood here where we now stand by the side of another man, led there by his destiny as you have been led here by yours.

"Then in one stoke he caught a wave and he was gone."

I wasn't surprised to see Uncle Hugh (or rather, his ghost). Because I knew in my heart of hearts that he would return to be by my side on this special day, as he had done so many times before—from horse shows to literary insecurities—to breathe life into me and prop up my sagging spirit.

For those of you who wonder why the dead return, there is only one explanation; they feel the strong pull of a loved one, who still needs them. Someday, I hope to be strong enough to really accept Uncle Hugh's death and set his spirit free, but not too far from Mon Plaisir.

What about happiness? I am happy, despite the fact that I'm still living on the borderline of two worlds: the world of skeletons in black robes, holding scythes, and the world of sunshine and flowers where angels sing in beautiful voices.

Yet there are times when laughter mingles with tears and I wonder about the true meaning of happiness. In the words of H. L. Mencken: "Happiness is probably only a passing accident. For a moment or two the organism is irritated so little that it is not conscious of it; for the duration of the moment it is happy. Thus a hog is always happier than a man, and a bacillus is happier than a hog."

In 1948, winter came early, bringing with it bucketfuls of rain and hail. The fury of nature created hazardous road conditions as early as October. It was during one of those rains when the wind beats its way through trees and the water rushes down from gutters with a ferocious force, mixing water and mud into a raging river, that it happened. Wait. I'm getting ahead of myself again.

During San Stefano's halcyon days there were very few cars in the village, certainly not enough to frighten the native dogs and cats. They literally had the run of the entire countryside. There was this funny dog, the size of a small Border Collie that had grown very attached to Percy's car. It knew that every Thursday Percy went to the Breaker, a smoky watering hole near the harbor breakwall. So it waited along the road for the car to appear. You see, it was Percy's habit to throw a piece of meat to the dog as a reward for its friendship.

On that particular Thursday, I was home alone curled up in front of the fireplace devouring a book. The dancing flames cast a warm red glow on the parquet flooring, reminiscent of a summer's sunrise. I heard the doorbell ring, but I was reluctant to give up my tenure in the pleasant idleness. At the second ring I opened the door. To my great surprise there stood a police officer wetter than a drowned cat. "I'm here to inform you that there was an accident. I believe the man in the car is your husband. But he is okay."

At once I wrapped myself with a rainproof cape and together we staggered into the darkness and water up to our ankles.

According to the police the cause of the accident was the heavy rain with sheets of obscuring water. The culprit: a homeless mongrel dog. Little did the police know that the dog in question was none other than the dog that loved Percy's car. Perhaps on that stormy night it lost its way and ran in front of the car? That one misjudgment caused Percy's car to flip onto its side and go off the road, where it crashed into a stone bridge, and landed in a ditch.

Despite the extensive damage to Percy's car, he himself escaped with only a few bruises and cuts. That's when I came to the conclusion that God must have been riding with him during the blizzard. There is no other explanation. Because the doctor told me the injuries could have been more serious—like losing a leg, an arm, an eye, or worse yet, his life.

I was so wrapped up in Percy's welfare that I failed to check on the dog lying in a large puddle of water. It didn't occur to me until many hours later that I had no idea whether or not the dog had survived the crash. To this day whenever I see a pack of dogs—the kind to be found in almost every village in Istanbul—a kaleidoscope of feelings sweep over me: concern, shame, guilt and fear as I feel two amber eyes glaring at me.

On the flyleaf of my new diary I wrote: What will happen tomorrow? I confessed to my diary that I had not always been honest with it. Eagerly I sought new ways to tell my journal that I loved two men: my husband Percy; who makes me tremendously happy, and my Uncle Hugh, who is a passion I cannot explain. He is all around me like a bright flame. I know it is impossible to stop loving Uncle Hugh, because it was he who first showed me a glimpse of heaven. It seems so natural to me that I should love them equally.

Just thinking about the ways of my destiny makes me chuckle at God's sense of humor.

And I don't think it is too dramatic to say that there is an offspring developing in my body. Somewhere deep in my heart someone is ringing a little bell that echoes it's a boy. We named him Hugh. Imagine that.

Read on for a preview of ...

The Mystery of the Silver Box,
another thrilling novel by Nikki Elst

On May 5, 1887, in the early hours of the morning, as a crystalline dawn descended over the grassy savanna, a pearl-skinned young woman, with clusters of waterfall curls falling from under her narrow-brimmed hat, stepped from the steamship *Leopold I* at Zanzibar City, Zanzibar, Africa. Despite the marvelous sight of the silver thread of water curving and twining through the harbor, creases of worry spread across her forehead as she felt hundreds of dark eyes upon her.

With a stone-cold stoicism and with a limited repertoire of Swahili she asked the directions for the Belgian Consulate in a cultured tone of voice. Her pale face was expressionless, she neither smiled nor displayed any form of emotion. Her soulful big eyes, emphasized by heavy eye makeup, were fixed on the baby lying in her arms, wrapped in a gossamer-fringed shawl.

The woman took a gulp of water and, with a lacy handkerchief, shooed away the flies swarming over the baby's head. Zanzibar's strange beauty lifted her spirits momentarily. Then, the realization that she was, indeed, in Zanzibar, the island state of the Omani Sultan, off the East Coast of Africa, shocked her into sobriety and she was glad to get into a carriage and get away from the bustle and busy life of the waterfront.